Layla smirked. "Thanks for the offer, Justin. I'll see you around."

He smiled at what was obviously a lie, since she was going to take great efforts not to see him, and took a step back. "Yeah. Layla. Sounds good."

Layla barely got outside the door when the words he'd said sunk in. She'd given as good as she'd got.

Hadn't she? Hmm. Maybe she hadn't.

She turned and knocked. When Justin opened the door, she took both sides of his face, pulled his head down and kissed him.

"What was that for?" he said when she finally let him go.

"That was for every time I've taken the high road and didn't respond in kind to all the stuff you and my brothers did to me."

He rubbed his thumb over his lower lip. "I like the way you retaliate."

Dear Reader,

Layla Taylor has long believed that if she planned well enough, her life would be safe, organized and secure—the exact opposite of the way she was raised. But when both her career and her love life evaporate within a matter of days, she begins to suspect that she's wasted time chasing goals because she thought she had to, not because she wanted to. She's determined to loosen up and enjoy life, but old habits are hard to break.

Enter Layla's childhood nemesis, chef Justin Tremont, the guy who ran her bra up the ROTC flagpole fifteen years ago. Justin is the last person Layla thought she'd use as a role model, but who better to teach her to loosen up than someone who lives for a good time?

Justin, however, is not the carefree guy he pretends to be, because he has a secret. The kind of secret that doesn't go away. The kind of secret that eats at a guy and eventually keeps him from forming long-term relationships. He's getting a kick out of the new Layla and is more than happy to help her loosen up a little—until he starts to suspect that Layla deserves a whole lot more than he's able to give.

Just Desserts is a book about acceptance—accepting the mistakes you've made, accepting that life isn't something that can be planned and controlled. Accepting that sometimes you just have to take a chance and hope for the best.

I enjoy hearing from readers. Please feel free to contact me at jeanniewrites@gmail.com, or visit my website, www.jeanniewatt.com.

Jeannie Watt

Just Desserts
Jeannie Watt

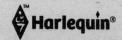

TORONTO NEW YORK LONDON
AMSTERDAM PARIS SYDNEY HAMBURG
STOCKHOLM ATHENS TOKYO MILAN MADRID
PRAGUE WARSAW BUDAPEST AUCKLAND

Recycling programs
for this product may
not exist in your area.

ISBN-13: 978-0-373-60685-6

JUST DESSERTS

Copyright © 2012 by Jeannie Steinman

www.Harlequin.com

Printed in U.S.A.

ABOUT THE AUTHOR

Jeannie Watt lives off the grid in rural Nevada and loves nothing better than an excellent meal. Jeannie is blessed with a husband who cooks more than she does, a son who knows how to make tapas and a daughter who knows the best restaurants in San Francisco. Her idea of heaven is homemade macaroni and cheese.

Books by Jeannie Watt

HARLEQUIN SUPERROMANCE

*Too Many Cooks?

Other titles by this author available in ebook format

To Jamie, baker of delicious cakes and other fattening treats, too numerous to name.

To Victoria, my most patient editor,

Thank you!

CHAPTER ONE

LAYLA TAYLOR WASN'T DRUNK enough to be hallucinating, which meant that Justin Tremont was not a figment of her imagination. Her childhood nemesis and the sworn enemy of all she held dear was indeed standing in the doorway of the Lake Tahoe lounge, scanning the room.

Crap.

She ducked her head, hoping he wouldn't see her drowning her sorrows, alone, as she waited for her sister to come pick her up. The lounge was dimly lit and crowded. There was no reason he *should* notice her, but less than a minute later she felt the vinyl bench give way beneath his weight as he sat beside her.

This evening just kept getting better.

"Hi, Layla," he said, when she cut him

a sideways glance. "I'm here to take you home."

"Over my dead body."

"Whatever."

Layla leaned her head back against the black vinyl booth cushion, noting with some alarm that when she closed her eyes, the room began to spin.

"Why are you here?" she asked without opening her eyes, certain that if she concentrated hard enough, she could make the spinning stop. Besides, she didn't need to see to know exactly what Justin was doing—smirking at her. Just as he'd smirked at her for her entire life. Well, not all of it. Only the ten years they'd lived down the street from each other, and her younger brothers and Justin, who were all a year behind her in school, had enjoyed some kind of an outlaw bond. The three of them had made her life miserable whenever possible.

"Sam called," Justin said, bringing her back to her very real problem at hand—him. "She asked me to take you home when I got off shift."

She'd called her sister to rescue her, and Sam had got Justin to come. Was no one in her entire family responsible?

Easy answer there. No.

She was going to kill her sister.

Layla opened her eyes to find Justin studying her with a slight frown, as if assessing her condition. She didn't like being assessed by Justin.

"Go home," she said, the last word slurring slightly. She wasn't going to tolerate any more smirking or misery at his hands. If he thought for one blinking second that she was going to allow him to be party to yet another of her humiliations, and drive her back to Reno…well, he could kiss her ass.

"I fully intend to do just that. Once I deliver *you* home as per Sam's orders."

Sam could kiss her ass, too.

Layla attempted to fix him with her teacher stare, the one that could melt a kid at twenty paces. Big mistake, because in doing so she had to focus, and that caused a dull pain to shoot through the front of her forehead, and her vision to waver. She clamped a hand to her head before she realized what she was doing.

"You know Sam wouldn't have asked me to give you a ride unless it was an emergency."

What in Sam's life wasn't an emergency? That was how her siblings—and her parents, for that matter—seemed to live, rebounding between emergencies. As if it energized them, for Pete's sake. She was, without a doubt, adopted. There was no way she shared DNA with her family.

"You want to help? Call me a cab."

"Are you kidding? From the lake to Reno? You don't make that kind of money." He stretched his arm out along the back of the booth, his fingertips making light contact with her shoulder.

Layla let out a breath. The connection actually felt kind of good. As if she wasn't alone in all this. But she was halfway drunk and her perceptions were not to be trusted. She didn't move any farther away, though, because that would have meant she cared.

"What happened with Sam?" she asked

resignedly. Hopefully, not something that would require Layla to bail her out.

"It's snowing pretty hard. Didn't you know? There's no way her little car will make it up here and back unless she's right on a snowplow's ass."

Spring in the Sierras. Great.

"There wasn't much coming down when we drove up," Layla muttered. The wet flakes had melted off the pavement as rapidly as they'd fallen. But if it was snowing hard now, then Sam's small Ford Escort wouldn't be safe on the road, and Justin probably had some kind of vehicle that could handle icy conditions. A vehicle she would not be getting into. "I'm fine here," she said. "I'll just get a room."

"Sold out. The Mind Breakers. Remember?"

"Trying to forget." The concert was the reason she was there. Layla took the stem of the empty martini glass between her thumb and forefinger, spinning it slowly as she thought. "Robert had a room for us," she muttered. Robert the blackheart.

"What happened with Robert?"

"He's sleeping with some trollop who works with me." Layla couldn't believe she'd just said that. That was it for martinis. The room was spinning. Her mouth was out of control. She shoved the glass across the table. Justin picked it up and set it on the tray of a passing bar server, who smiled at him and asked if he wanted another.

"We'll pass," Justin said, easing his hip up to pull out his wallet. He set a bill on the tray.

"Thanks," the woman said with a pert smile that made Layla want to smack her for some reason. "See you around, Tremont."

Layla half turned in the booth to face Justin. She was going to try a new tactic. "I do appreciate you offering to take me home, but I'm just going to sit here for a while. My head will clear and then I'll figure out how I want to handle this. It's really none of your business." It took her longer to make the speech than expected, since some of the words tangled her tongue. But she got it out, and Justin, to her relief, slid from the booth.

"Fine."

Really? Oh, please let it be that easy.

"Remember how Derek used to practice for his fireman test?"

Layla's eyes widened. "You wouldn't…."

Justin simply tilted his head.

How could she have even asked such a stupid question? Of course he would. Justin loved nothing more than a dare.

"Leave me alone!" she said with sudden venom. "I don't want you to rescue me."

"Why?" he asked with a touch of weariness.

"Why? Because of all the crummy things you've done to me."

His eyes narrowed thoughtfully. "Name one."

He looked as if he didn't think she could. He was so wrong. Layla drew a deep breath and fought the fog in her brain. "You…picked on me as a kid."

He appeared unimpressed by the generic description of his actions, so she searched her brain for the perfect representative incident. There were so many to choose from. Finally, she stabbed a finger at him. "You talked my date out of going to the prom with me."

Justin gave a soft snort. "He was a jerk."

Maybe so. She pointed at him again. "You put a frog in my lunch bag." The lunchroom had been packed when she'd let out a bloodcurdling scream as her bag started to move.

Justin shrugged.

Another stab of the finger. "You ran my bra up the ROTC flagpole. You glued my English comp book shut. You put pudding in my slippers. You…you…" Had done so many small things she couldn't remember them all.

"Do you want an apology?" he asked quietly. "For all the many wrongs you've suffered at my hands? Then would you come with me?"

"An apology wouldn't suffice."

"Good. Because I'm not sorry for most of it." He placed one palm flat on the table and leaned his face close to hers, so close that she could see tiny flecks of navy blue in his green eyes. "Now get your stuff so we can start home before the real blizzard hits."

"If you don't leave," Layla said between clenched teeth, "I'm going to call security." Or someone.

"Go ahead," Justin replied. "No, wait. I'll do it." He straightened and glanced across the lobby to the uniformed man standing near the slot machines. When Justin raised a hand and gestured, the security guard started toward them.

"You will regret this," Layla said with a slight smile. Because she was *not* as drunk as he seemed to think.

"Hey, how's it going," the guard said, breaking into a smile as he clapped Justin on the arm.

Layla groaned.

"The wife was so happy with the anniversary party," Mr. Security continued. "She told me she was glad we went with you guys instead of the other caterer she'd chosen. For once *I* was right."

"Great," Justin said, smiling back. "I

was wondering if you have any of the emergency hotel rooms available."

"Robert has a room," Layla muttered. "But I am *not* staying there." Justin touched her back reassuringly as the guard shook his head.

"Not one. Mind Breakers are big."

"So," Justin continued smoothly, "if Ms. Taylor here is feeling a bit…ill, it'd be best if I took her home?"

The guard's dark eyebrows drew together. "As opposed to…"

"Her hanging out somewhere in the hotel waiting to sober up?"

Oh, great mental picture. Layla stood abruptly, hitting her thigh on the edge of the table. It scooted sideways with a screech of metal on tile, and the room swam once she was vertical. She automatically reached out and clutched Justin's shoulder. It was either that or go down.

All her arguments about being fine and not needing him to butt into her life evaporated when the guard's face wavered in front of her. *Oh, boy.*

"Take her home, Justin," the man said.

Layla kept her mouth shut as she fought to regain her balance.

Justin settled a hand on her waist to help steady her, and she felt the warmth of his fingers through the thin silk of her black dress. But she didn't move away, because she couldn't.

Robert-1. Justin-1. Layla-0.

Double-teamed in the worst way. Hell, if she counted the gin, she'd been triple-teamed.

"Hey, Miss Taylor!" A teenage voice penetrated the fog and she moved her head to the left, focusing on the group of people passing in the hall, headed toward the concert venue. Students. Her students. She forced the corners of her mouth up, but was not so foolish as to try to speak. Or wave, since she was still hanging on to Justin.

She glanced down at the bench, wondering how a few feet of altitude could make her head spin so nastily. She had to do something. Mind Breakers *were* big and several of her rather privileged students were likely here in the hotel. Along with their deep-pocketed parents.

"Get me out of here," she muttered to Justin, without looking at him. "Please," she added, just to make her humiliation total and complete.

LAYLA WAS TRYING HARD TO WALK without leaning on him. She was losing the battle. Justin didn't know how many martinis she'd downed after receiving the happy news that her boyfriend was sleeping around, but he knew from experience that the bartenders at this particular hotel didn't play coy with the booze. They charged a lot for a drink and they delivered.

What Justin wanted to know was whether Robert had abandoned her at the bar after she'd found out he was sleeping with the "trollop," or if she'd stormed out of their room and taken refuge in the bar while waiting for Sam. Because if Robert had abandoned her, drunk as she was… well, Justin might have to do something about that.

They stepped out the front doors onto the freshly shoveled sidewalk. The snow had let up a little since he'd come into the hotel, but it wasn't done. Not by a long shot. Just a lull.

Layla clamped a hand to her stomach, and Justin stopped walking. If she was going to be sick, he'd prefer it wasn't in his car.

"I'm fine," she said in a brittle voice as she took a resolute step forward. Justin moved with her, only to have her stop dead a few seconds later and look around wildly. He steered her off the sidewalk, through the snow and as far around the giant juniper bush flanking the walkway as he could before she heaved. She swung at him when he tried to get hold of her hair, so he let go of her and stepped aside, allowing her to commune with the bush. When she sat back on her heels and drew in a shaky breath, he held out a hand. She clutched his fingers, allowed him to help her up, but she didn't look at him.

"I…feel a little better."

Justin shook his head and, after brushing the wet snow off her knees and the front of her black wool coat, helped her back to the sidewalk. People had paused to watch the spectacle, but now moved on. *Show's over, folks. Nothing to see here.*

He and Layla started for the car again, which was parked in the employee lot, even though Justin wasn't an employee of this particular hotel. Layla was walking better now that she'd emptied her stomach, and Justin hoped she had no memory of puking in the bush in front of a crowd, because, tight-ass that she was, she wouldn't be able to handle it.

"Layla!"

She stopped dead, her entire body going stiff at the sound of the man's voice calling her name. Then she turned with what sounded like a growl to face the guy jogging lightly toward them through the snow. He stopped a few feet away, eyeing Justin suspiciously. "Who are you?"

"Old family friend. Here to help pick up the pieces. You must be the Robert I've heard so much about."

"Is he?" Robert asked Layla. "A family friend?"

"Who he is…is none of your business," she said with an air of dignity and only the slightest slur.

Robert grimaced. "How much have you had to drink?"

Justin's jaw slid sideways and he took a step toward the guy. "Since you walked out on her, you mean?"

"I'm not talking to you."

"But I can't help hearing the conversation."

"I'm not going to have her driving off this mountain in a snowstorm with someone I don't know." Robert fished in his pocket. "I hadn't realized you didn't have the room key," he said to Layla, holding it out to her. "Take it. You can spend the night as planned. Your overnight bag is in the room."

Layla stared down at the plastic card, then slowly raised her eyes to Robert's face. He continued to hold the key, giving it a slight shake as if encouraging her to take it. She pulled in a breath that made her shoulders rise a good inch, then drew back her arm and punched him square in the jaw.

He stumbled backward as she lost her balance and went down. Justin made a grab for her, grunting when her elbow smacked into his cheekbone with a healthy crack.

"Oh, shit…" Tears sprang to his eyes as Layla slowly struggled to her hands and knees, and finally, her feet. She stared at Justin in horror as he stood with his hand over his eye. Five yards away, Robert held a hand to his nose.

"Oh, I'm sorry. So sorry." She continued to stare at Justin, a dazed expression on her face.

"Get out of here," he said to Robert, keeping his full attention on Layla, half-afraid of what she might do next. "Leave her bag in the room and I'll take care of it."

"I'm not—"

"I honestly am a family friend. I know her middle name and everything."

"What is it?" Robert asked through his

fingers, and Justin had to give him points for not abandoning her.

"Sunshine. Layla Sunshine Taylor."

"Brothers?"

"Twins—Eric and Derek. Sister is Sam. Formerly Belle Blue, from the song 'Bell Bottom Blues.' She renamed herself when she was five because the kids called her Ding Dong."

"Good enough." Robert turned and walked away without another word, still holding his nose.

"You didn't have to tell him all that," Layla said as Justin put a hand under her arm and steered her the last few feet to the Challenger—an adequate car, but a poor substitute for his classic Firebird, destroyed in a wreck last year.

"I think he already knew." Justin held the door open and she got into the passenger seat, then carefully arranged her coat over her knees. "Where do you live?"

She muttered an address on Bannock Drive. He made her repeat it, since it wouldn't be cool to drag her up the sidewalk of someone else's house. Then he asked for her keys.

"Why?"

"So that you have them when we get to your place."

With a deep sigh she spilled the contents of her purse onto her lap, then pulled the keys out of the jumble. She slapped them into his outstretched hand before haphazardly shoving stuff back into her bag.

Justin closed the door and walked around to his side of the car. By the time he got the beast started, Layla was leaning against the leather headrest and her eyes were closed. *Good.* He hoped she stayed that way during the entire trip.

It wasn't to be. She got sick again at the top of the grade leading down to Carson City, where, thankfully, it wasn't snowing. She was still a bit green when she collapsed back into the passenger seat and fell asleep.

Justin couldn't say he was unhappy about that because he wanted to focus on the road, not on his passenger. Nearly a year ago, he'd had a close call on this road, when fellow employees at his hotel who were involved in the drug trade erroneously deduced that he was a narc, due to his association with his current brother-in-law, a drug task force member. About a mile past the summit, Justin had been hit from behind, and his beloved classic Firebird sent plummeting down the ravine. He was so damned lucky to be alive, and he'd never felt the same driving this road. What's more, he missed his car.

Forty-five minutes after passing the spot where his car had been wrecked, Justin pulled into Layla's drive. He roused her and helped her out, then put an arm around her as they made their way through the slushy spring snow to the front door. Not a bad place. In fact, it was very much what he'd expected from Layla. An efficient box of a house, with neat little shutters, a sturdy fence in front, a no-nonsense white-and-navy-blue color scheme. The bushes were all trimmed into submission, even though it was barely spring.

There were only three keys on the ring, so he had her inside within a matter of seconds. Once the door was closed, she attempted to focus on him. The way her forehead wrinkled, it must have hurt.

She started to say something, but got only as far as opening her mouth before she shrugged out of her coat, letting it fall behind her in a heap. Then she headed down the hall.

Justin hesitated, then followed. By the time he reached her bedroom, she was sprawled on her stomach over the purple duvet on her bed. It looked like something that would need an expensive drycleaning if she were ill again, so Justin carefully peeled it back and rolled her onto her side on the sheets.

He stood for a moment then, his thumbs hooked in his pockets, staring down at her. He hadn't seen her in several years—not since her father had sold the house down the street from his family's, shortly after Justin graduated high school. She'd put on some weight. In a good way. And her straight dark hair was longer. But she was still Layla. Only not so perfect now. He hoped she could deal with it.

With a slight shrug of his shoulders, he set her keys on the dresser and headed out the bedroom door.

LAYLA DIDN'T WANT TO wake up.

Her head was pounding. Her mouth was dry. So dry! And why was she drowning in a sense of impending doom?

The memories started to drift in, each more cringe-worthy than the one before. Had she thrown up outside the hotel?

Worse than that, had Justin been there?

And then the biggie hit her. Robert. Robert and Melinda. Layla's insides roiled as a wave of depression mixed with pain, betrayal and disgust washed over her.

"You need anything?"

Layla shrieked at the unexpected masculine voice, and scrambled to her knees, ready to defend herself with the pillow she'd grabbed. "Justin!"

"Yeah. Me."

She lowered the pillow and sat back on her heels as a surge of nausea welled up.

But her stomach was too empty to do anything about it.

"Let me get you some aspirin. Where do you keep it?"

She simply stared at him. "Why are you here?"

"You can't leave a drunk person unattended. Remember what happened to all those rock stars that drowned in their own—"

Layla held up a hand. "Stop. No more." She dropped her head on the pillow she held in her lap. It made sense, really. Justin had been part of so many of the humiliating moments of her life that perhaps he was on call. He sensed "Layla devastation" and showed up to add to the misery.

"It was too late for Sam to come and stay with you."

Layla nodded, her head bobbing into the pillow. He had a point. He'd done the safe and logical thing.

"Thank you for bringing me home." She vaguely recalled trying to stay in the hotel until she sobered up. And students. She remembered seeing her students.

Her stomach flip-flopped at the thought. Hopefully, she hadn't appeared too out of it. Private schools were not very keen on their staff being seen drunk in public.

"Aspirin?"

Layla lifted her head. "I'll get it." She steeled herself for the trauma of going vertical. "What happened to your eye?" Another dim recollection was taking form in her brain.

"You punched Robert when he tried to give you the room key."

"Did I…punch you, too?" Had all her pent-up frustrations burst forth? Culminating in a brawl?

"No. You accidentally hit me when you fell."

Layla swallowed hard and looked down at her hands. Well, now she knew why her knuckles were bruised and her knees felt skinned.

"You can go home now, Justin." She was certain he probably couldn't wait to get out of there, even though seeing her like this was probably entertaining as could be. "Thanks for everything."

"All right." He stayed where he was, though, and for once he wasn't smirking. He looked tired.

"Where'd you sleep?" she finally asked, after a few beats of silence. For some reason, he wasn't leaving.

"In one of those baskets you call a chair." He leaned his shoulder against the door frame. "How many drinks did you have?"

"Three." Layla closed her eyes for a second, hugging the pillow to her chest, fighting the urge to topple over. "And a half," she added, for the sake of honesty.

"How many after Robert dropped the bomb?"

"I told you about that?" Had she no pride when intoxicated? Heat rose in her face, scalding her cheeks.

"I'm not a mind reader."

Layla felt like melting into a puddle on the bed. "He told me in the room when we were getting ready to go down to dinner." Actually, that wasn't quite true. She'd guessed and then he'd confessed. "I hid out in the lounge and called Sam."

"Just wondering if I need to hook up with this Robert guy for leaving you drunk and alone in a hotel lounge."

The last thing she wanted was for Justin, of all people, to defend her honor. That would be so wrong.

"Justin…I'd really like to be alone now."

"If you're sure you're okay."

"I'm okay." He cocked his head, and she added, "Physically." Obviously, she had some other nonphysical issues to deal with.

That seemed to satisfy him, and a few seconds later the front door closed. She heard the purr of a powerful engine coming to life.

What had they driven home in?

She couldn't for the life of her remember. Perhaps because her memory was so jumbled with other more humiliating images. The bush outside the hotel came to mind. And…oh, yeah. She'd tossed her cookies once again along a road somewhere.

What did they put in those drinks?

Lots and lots of alcohol. And she was a lightweight.

She gingerly crawled off the bed, realizing only then that she still had on her slightly damp T-strap high heels. Justin hadn't taken off her shoes, although he had removed the duvet cover. Well, they were buckle shoes, perhaps too complicated for him.

She'd started for the bathroom when the doorbell rang. What on earth had Justin forgotten? She glanced at the domed mantel clock on her way to the door. Ten-thirty? Criminy. She'd lost twelve hours of her life.

The doorbell rang again, the sound reverberating through her skull. Must disconnect that thing. She pulled the door open, about to ask, "What did you forget?" and then almost slammed it shut again as she found herself facing the sweet, round face of Kristy Mendoza, the girl who lived next door.

CHAPTER TWO

KRISTY'S MOUTH DROPPED OPEN, as did her mother's. But Mrs. Mendoza, who stood a few feet behind the girl, managed a polite, if wary, smile.

"I have the cookies you ordered," Kristy said abruptly, shoving the box forward.

Layla took them. Smiled. Resisted the urge to look down and see what her very expensive black silk cocktail dress, perfect for a night out in Tahoe, looked like after being slept in. "Thank you, Kristy."

"Are you all right?" the girl blurted out before her mother clamped a hand on her shoulder and squeezed. Hard, judging from the way she winced.

"I'll get my wallet," Layla said, hoping she had five bucks. "Just a sec." She left the door open in spite of the cold and turned to find her purse in one of the living-room chairs. She dug through the contents. Frowned. Dug again, then dumped everything out.

"Uh, that's all right," Mrs. Mendoza called.

"No, really. I have the money."

"You can run it over when you find it. We have more deliveries to make. Come on, Kristy...*Kristy!*"

"No, wait..." Layla called. She really didn't want to face these two later today.

But it was too late. Mrs. Mendoza was already guiding her daughter firmly down the sidewalk toward safety. Layla sighed and shut the door, the click of the lock making her head throb.

After another futile search for the wallet in her coat pockets, she headed for the bathroom and faced her reflection with a sick feeling growing inside her stomach.

She was a raccoon. A punk raccoon with ratted hair, and wearing morning-after clothes.

What? What had she ever done to deserve all this?

Dated Robert Baldwin?

Her stomach twisted and she was afraid she was going to be sick again.

JUSTIN PARKED IN THE ALLEY behind Tremont Catering and sat in his car for a minute before turning off the engine. Hell of a night. Well, the next two days weren't going to be any kind of a picnic, either, so maybe it was just as well to tune up on an unrelated event. Tomorrow marked the tenth anniversary of the day he'd signed the papers that had changed his life, and even though he'd been happy at the time, now he wondered if he'd made the right choice. If he should have pursued other options....

Not that there was anything he could do about it now.

Justin let himself in the back door of the kitchen, where the smell of tomato sauce instantly hit him. It was Sunday and his sister Eden, who moonlighted as a personal chef in addition to her duties with Tremont Catering, would thankfully be busy making a week's worth of meals for her client families—one of which she'd cooked for since beginning the business and the other brand-new, replacing the family she'd lost after her fiancé discovered they were involved in the drug trade. A tough chapter in both Eden and Justin's lives.

His eye was still throbbing where Layla had decked him, and he couldn't say he was in the best of moods after spending a nearly sleepless night at her house. Hell, he could have easily stretched out on the bed beside her and been comfortable, but knowing his luck she would have woken up and smacked him again.

If only she'd had a sofa…which made him contemplate just what kind of person didn't own a sofa. Well, Layla wasn't your normal type.

He stifled a yawn as he came into the main kitchen area after kicking off his street shoes and putting on his clogs. He didn't spend as much time standing in front of a stove as his sisters, but still put in long hours on his feet, creating every flower known to man, and some that weren't, out of butter cream and a piping bag.

It was a living, and fortunately, since he spent so much time at it, one that he enjoyed.

"You're here early," Eden muttered when she looked up from the stove. She blinked when she saw his eye, which had swollen up nicely, but asked no questions. That was a sad commentary on how many times she'd found him in a similar condition throughout their lives.

"Fight in a parking lot," Justin said. "And no, I wasn't drunk."

"Well, you look like hell."

"I feel like hell." He wandered over to the stove, breathing in the savory smell of his sister's homemade tomato sauce.

"Where's the oregano?" he asked.

"Going straight basil this time."

"You shouldn't mess with perfection." His sister used a perfect blend of oregano, thyme and basil in her sauces.

"There's always room for improvement."

Indeed. Justin never stopped trying to improve his technique.

Eden started chopping olives again. "Where'd you have your fight?"

"The lake. It was more of a scuffle, really. I caught an elbow."

"No arrests?"

"Not that I know of. Then I drove Layla Taylor home and stayed with her for most of the night to make sure she was okay."

The rapid movement of Eden's knife had abruptly stopped around the time Justin said Layla's name.

"Run that by me again," his sister demanded.

"All of it?"

"No. Just the Layla Taylor part." Eden set the knife down and brushed her blond hair off her forehead with the back of her wrist. "None of this makes sense."

"Sam Taylor called me at the lake and asked me to give Layla a ride. We had a minor altercation in the parking lot with her ex-boyfriend, then she puked and I took her home." It wasn't quite the right order, but Justin didn't think the chronology mattered.

"She puked because she was…"

"Drunk as hell."

"Layla? Drunk?"

"Mmm-hmm. And for once it wasn't with power." Justin went into his pastry room and took a look at the list he'd left himself the night before. He didn't turn on the music because he knew it wouldn't be long before—

"I want details," Eden said, leaning her shoulder against the door frame.

"I wish I had some. I don't."

"Wow." She processed his words for a moment, then slowly turned and went back into the kitchen, deep in thought. Even though he and his sisters had grown up up the street from the Taylors, neither Eden nor their older sister, Reggie, had ever warmed up to Layla, probably because she had nothing to do with anyone in their neighborhood. Reggie had thought Layla was pretty damned stuck up back in the day, which was saying something, since Reggie hadn't been the warmest of people herself then. After their mother had died, their father took more and more long haul truck jobs, basically leaving the kids to fend for themselves. Reggie had been too busy running the household in their father's absence to socialize, and too angry at his abandonment to be particularly warm and fuzzy to anyone.

Eden reappeared in the doorway. "I forgot—Cindy stopped by yesterday." Justin continued to study the list. "She dropped off a bag of clothes. Your clothes. It's in the laundry room. She'll get the key back to you when she picks up her stuff."

"Thanks." He didn't quite meet his sister's eyes.

"What happened?"

"Things just didn't work out."

"Damn, Justin. You finally date a girl I like and—"

"You suddenly feel a deep need to mind your own business?" he asked.

Eden wasn't in the least insulted or deterred. "I thought she was perfect for you."

Yes, Cindy had been practically perfect. She worked in a downtown restaurant. They understood each other's occupations; they'd had a lot of fun. And that

was as far as he would let it go. He didn't
know why, wasn't a huge believer in self-
analysis, but once a relationship hit a certain point, he was done. Just…done.

His relationship with Cindy had hit that
point.

"You're going to run out of compati-
ble women," Eden warned before heading
back into the kitchen.

"Reno's a big town and lots of people
move here every day," Justin called after
her.

Eden came back a few seconds later
with a calendar showing the events for the
week. "Okay. Patty has her surgery set for
next Wednesday, and it looks like you'll
be on your own for the next six weeks."

Justin reached up to adjust his stocking
hat. "I told the hotel I can't be called in for
any emergencies for a while." After hiring
on as a prep cook at Tremont, Patty had,
for some reason, made his work her pri-
ority, and he'd come to depend on her—
which allowed him to take extra work at
the lake and make more specialty cakes
than he'd been able to before.

"That's the sanest thing you've said in months," Eden muttered. She placed the calendar on the counter between them. "You're working the parties on Tuesday night and Wednesday night, right?"

"Right. And that business brunch at the lake tomorrow." After that, he was holing up for the evening.

"Okay." She laid the list on his stainless-steel counter. "Here's the desserts we'll need for the bookings this week and next...." Her voice trailed off and she looked up at him with a slight frown. "I am having the hardest time visualizing you and Layla fighting in the parking lot."

"Don't forget the boyfriend. He was there, too."

"Strange." She gave her head a slight shake, then pointed back at the list. "Seven dozen cherry bomb mini cupcakes for the tea on Thursday—"

The phone in Justin's pocket vibrated, making him jump. It was the Tremont cell, not his own, that he was carrying. "Tremont Catering. Justin here."

"Uh, hi." The voice was hoarse, feminine and distinct.

"Layla?" Justin said, rather enjoying the way Eden's head snapped up.

"Would you mind checking your car to see if my wallet fell out in there? Because if it didn't, then I have another headache to deal with."

She was probably dealing with a whopper already.

"Sure thing. Stay on the line and I'll check right now." He walked past Eden and out the back door without saying a word into the phone, because he really couldn't think of anything to say. He opened the passenger door, dug around under the seat, then shoved his hand deep into the crack between the seats and struck gold.

"Got it," he said, pulling out a slim eelskin wallet. "You must have lost it when you dumped your purse out."

"I dumped my…never mind. Thank you for finding it."

"I'm pretty swamped today, but I can drop it by your house on my way home."

"Don't bother. I'll pick the wallet up tomorrow on my way to work."

"It'll be here waiting for you." And Justin wouldn't be. "I'm going to the lake tomorrow for a catering event. I, uh, could pick up your overnight bag there if you want."

"Oh." It was obvious she hadn't even thought about that. And that she wanted to say no, but wasn't going to. "Thank you. I would very much appreciate it."

He smiled at her stiff tone. Likely she was torn between gratitude and a desire to keep him out of her life. "You know me, Layla—always there to lend a hand."

There was a slight choking sound and then the phone went dead.

SAM, WHO COULDN'T MAKE IT up to the lake in her little car to rescue Layla, did make it across town just fine to see her sister on her way to the small shop she ran a few blocks from Layla's house. But in Sam's defense, the snow that had pelted the mountains was a slushy sleet in Reno.

"Oh. My." Sam stopped dead in the

doorway and stared at her sister for a long moment, oblivious to the wet snow blowing into the house. Layla grabbed her by the sleeve and tugged her inside.

"I haven't had time to shower."

"Well, at least wipe the mascara from under your eyes."

Layla nodded. But she didn't move.

Sam's eyes grew wide. "This is bad, isn't it?"

"I don't think I've ever had a worse day than yesterday."

"Considering some of the stuff the twins did to you, that's saying a lot."

Layla nodded again, then sat on the upholstered window seat. She hadn't changed out of her dress, hadn't managed to do much of anything except to lie quivering on her bed, fighting the mother of all hangovers. She did feel slightly better now that the Pepto Bismol and aspirin had taken effect. Physically, anyway.

"Tell me about it," Sam said, sitting beside her.

Layla turned to her sister, who was so very different from her, and took in the

short red hair, the fuchsia lipstick painted
into an exaggerated Cupid's bow, the
clothes that appeared more costumelike
than conventional. Yes, they were from
different planets, but if anyone was going
to understand… She took a deep breath
and the story poured out. One solid hit to
her ego and self-dignity after another.

"I knew something was…off," Layla
said, talking to her clasped hands. "For
weeks.

"He took you to the lake to tell you he
was sleeping with someone else."

Layla looked up at her sister. "No. I
asked him why we hadn't—" she gestured
"—you know…slept together much lately.
And then I jokingly asked if he was wearing himself out with someone else." She
bit her lip as she recalled the way the color
had drained from his face. "He was. Is."
She shook her hair back. "Melinda. From
school."

"Melinda!"

"They met at the school faculty Christmas party."

"That bitch!"

"I introduced them." She'd rather smugly wanted Melinda, who was always jockeying for top position at the school, to see what kind of a great guy she, Layla, had landed. Joke was on her.

"That has to sting." Sam put an arm around her shoulders and Layla gave up the fight, slumping against her. She didn't let herself depend on people often. She'd been disappointed so many times in the past by her well-meaning but easily distracted family. But right now, for this moment, she was going to lean on her sister. Literally and figuratively.

The closeness lasted almost two seconds before Sam said, "I have to get down to the store and unpack a shipment. Want to come?"

"Is it regular gifts or...?"

"It's *or*," Sam said with a half smile. "Some funky new stuff. And lingerie. It'll take your mind off..." Her voice trailed away as she apparently realized sexy lingerie was not going to take Layla's mind off Robert sleeping with someone else. "Or not," she added weakly.

Layla smiled. Kind of. "Any other time, yes, but right now I just want to wallow in misery for a while. Nurse my head."

"I understand. Do you want me to make you some tea and Pop-Tarts before I go? I have strawberry in my bag." Sam lifted her giant tote, which probably had a couple boxes of toaster pastries in it. Her sister lived on them.

Layla's stomach flip-flopped. "No, thanks. I'm still feeling a bit queasy."

"I wish I'd been able to get you last night, but there was no way the Escort could have made it up the pass."

"I know."

"And Justin was there."

"Oh, that he was." And he was here in the morning, too. "It all worked out as well as it could have." Except maybe for Justin, who had a black eye. Normally she might have enjoyed that, but not under these circumstances. Besides, she was too old to get delight out of Justin being on the receiving end of some well-deserved retribution.

Well, almost too old.

"Next shipment, I promise I'll help." It was usually entertaining to unpack the stuff her sister sold. If nothing else, Layla got a good laugh.

Sam stood up and wrapped her mile of hand-knit scarf around her neck. Somehow she managed to pull off funky without looking like a cartoon. If Layla had tried to wear a lace smock over a striped T-shirt with skinny jeans and over-the-knee boots, she would have resembled a wannabe pirate. Sam looked comfortable and stylish.

"Want me to stop by on my way home?"

"No need. But thanks for propping me up."

"First time."

It quite possibly was. Layla felt as if she were living in Bizarro World all of a sudden.

THE NEXT MORNING Layla woke up feeling almost human—physically, anyway. Mentally, she wasn't doing so hot.

In less than an hour, she had to go to school, face Melinda. March through her day as if nothing was wrong, and wonder how many people knew about Robert and Melinda's extracurricular activities. Was this a classic case of the girlfriend being the last to know? She hoped not.

No doubt Robert had warned Melinda that the gig was up—after all, he had to explain his sore nose somehow. As she did her makeup, Layla wondered how perfect Melinda would react.

Hopefully she'd do the sane thing and avoid Layla—for the next several years, if possible. Except they worked in the same building—the same hall—and sooner or later had to interact, which made Layla believe that the one blessing of this situation, other than finally discovering that Robert was a rat, was the timing. There would be no student witnesses to any stiff conversations between herself and Melinda, since the term had just ended and school was on hiatus for three weeks. Technically, it was also a teacher vacation after tomorrow, the second of two mandatory workdays, but most people came in for at least a few more days during the March break. Nothing was said aloud, but upper administration expected extra hours, and Layla, who'd dreamed of being a teacher since she was a small child, gave them exactly what they wanted. As did Melinda.

Which meant it would be one hell of a hiatus.

Layla pulled a conservative navy blue blouse and pleated khaki pants from her closet, paired the outfit with black loafers and a heart locket, and then paused to consider her reflection in the cheval mirror. Oh, yes. She looked wonderfully frumpy. Exactly like the kind of woman who'd get dumped. All she needed was a droopy mom cardigan to complete the picture.

Maybe she should do something about her teacherific wardrobe.

And maybe, instead of spending her vacation at the school, she'd be better off holing up and healing a bit. She needed to gain strength and perspective. It wasn't as if she hadn't spent hundreds of extra hours at the school since being hired three years ago.

Except that all Manzanita teachers put in hundreds of extra unpaid hours and the upper administration would notice if she didn't.

Layla stopped by Tremont Catering, having looked up the location on the internet. A short woman with curly brown hair handed her the wallet with a quick "Have a nice day," and Layla headed off to school, glad that Justin hadn't been there to hand over the wallet personally.

Perhaps this was a sign that her life was edging back to normal. Or not. The second she walked past the open office door, the secretary hailed her and told her that the principal wanted a word.

Layla's stomach dropped, but she forced a smile and went into Ella Murdock's office.

"Close the door," Ella said, seated behind her broad oak desk. "We need to discuss this." She turned her computer monitor slightly so that Layla could see the photo that filled the screen—of Layla, on her knees…vomiting.

Not a pretty picture in any sense of the word.

Layla put a hand to her chest and forced her mouth shut. She felt like throwing up again.

"You didn't know." Ella fixed her with a quelling look. The principal was too well-bred to actually say, "What the hell were you thinking?" but if she had, Layla wouldn't have known or cared, because she was approaching a catatonic state.

After a very long, very silent moment, she tried to moisten her lips, but her mouth was so dry it was impossible. She cleared her throat. Her head throbbed as blood pounded through her skull. "Oh, dear," she said numbly, thinking it was best to let Ella direct the conversation—at least until her brain recovered enough to do some quick thinking.

"This appeared on Facebook. A concerned parent called me. Do you *have* an explanation?"

"I, uh, became ill when I was leaving the hotel at Lake Tahoe?"

"Food poisoning?"

"That's what it felt like." Not really a lie.

Ella nodded. "That's exactly what I've told the half dozen parents who have emailed me concerning this photo."

"Are they buying it?" Layla asked, her stomach knotting at the idea of parents contacting Ella about her. She'd always been so careful to behave in an exemplary way. Coming from the freewheeling lifestyle her family reveled in, she was doubly careful to stay within boundaries, color inside the lines.

"Short of running a toxicology test on the residue, what choice do they have?" Ella asked with a sniff. "*I* told them it was food poisoning." Her lips thinned as she pressed them together. "See that it doesn't happen again."

She didn't need to remind Layla that at the end of this year, her annual contract might not be renewed. Private school contracts went year to year and she had no union to negotiate for her—the price she paid for teaching the best and the brightest.

"I appreciate your support," Layla said. She swallowed and then asked, "Is that the…only photo?"

"Might there be more?" Ella asked in a deadly voice.

Layla instantly shook her head. "I didn't even know about this one. I just don't want any more nasty surprises." Such as a photo of her taking a swing at her ex in a parking lot. Her hands were clenched into tight fists and she forced them to relax. Surely if there'd been more pictures, they would have made their way onto Facebook, as well.

"Neither do I," Ella said coolly.

"I didn't do anything wrong," Layla stated. For a brief moment she thought about telling her exactly what had happened and why, but that wasn't the principal's concern. Layla was not going to pour her troubles out to her boss, especially when the woman was going to bat for her with the concerned parents—and when it might make her wonder if Layla and Melinda could continue to work together. "But I want to apologize for all the trouble you're going to on my behalf."

Ella's expression remained serious. "I hope it's enough." Layla didn't even want to think about what that meant. It had to be enough. "Time is on our side," the principal continued. "Memories are short, and by the time the break is over and the students come back, this will probably be long forgotten."

Layla was certainly happy that she'd screwed up at the perfect time.

Ella smiled slightly, her dismissal. "I think everything will be fine."

Layla nodded in agreement and left. Everything *would* be fine—except for the part where she and Melinda had to share the same air. Conniving bitch.

But Robert was to blame, too.

Conniving son of a bitch. In many ways she blamed him more, because Melinda couldn't help herself. She was wired to be cute and competitive, to be the winner at all costs, in all forums. Everyone knew that.

Layla hurried down the hall to her room, glad that the building was, for the most part, still empty. Teachers at Manzanita tended to work late rather than come in early, except for a few diehards. The light was on in Mr. Coppersmith's room, but there were rumors that he never went home. Ever. Layla tried to recall a time she'd arrived before him or stayed after him, and couldn't come up with one. Melinda's room, two doors down from Layla's, was dark, and so was Sandy Albright's, directly across the hall. Safe. For now.

Layla fitted her key into the lock, felt the smooth click and let herself inside, closing the door behind her. Then for a moment she simply stood, tote bag with lesson plans and books in one hand, her purse in the other, studying her desk, neat as always. The student work posted on the back bulletin board. The walls she'd painted pale blue herself on her own dime, after reading that the color fostered creativity.

She'd worked so hard to get here, into this posh private academy, and she worked equally hard to stay here. Yes, she got headaches and stomachaches worrying about her job, but that was the price she paid for having students actively working to achieve their destinies. Students who wanted to learn. They were for the most part a privileged lot, special and well aware of it, but they were also just kids.

And one of them had probably snapped her photo in the Lake Tahoe parking lot and then posted it on Facebook for all to see.

Which one?

Did it really matter?

Layla turned on the light and left the door locked so that no one could pop in on her without knocking—just in case she had another crazy bout of tears once the numbness wore off and the ramifications of having that photo posted set in.

Thankfully, no one was foolish enough

to attempt to enter her room that morning, although Layla could hear people in the hall. Was Melinda one of them?

Were people talking about her?

Layla had never been the subject of gossip before and she sincerely hoped she wasn't now, but the words *fat* and *chance* kept circling through her mind.

She ate her lunch alone at her desk, slipped out unseen twice to use the ladies' room, then scuttled back for cover. If she could make it through today, then she'd be able to face the faculty meeting tomorrow. She just didn't feel quite steady yet, didn't trust herself to be able to look into Melinda's face and smile as if she didn't care about what had happened.

But her solitary, strength-building day ended with a call from Ella just before the final minutes of the school day ticked to an end.

"Please see me before you leave."

"I'll be right down."

Layla's stomach tightened the minute she saw the older woman's expression. Trouble. Possibly big trouble.

"It appears we have a situation," Ella said. "Your photo has gone viral, I believe the term is, and parents have been calling all day. Apparently several students attending the concert at the hotel saw you 'draped' over a man, barely able to walk, you were so intoxicated."

"Or ill."

"They aren't buying it, and because of that, because of the particular parents who have been calling with concerns…to mollify…" Ella pulled in a deep breath. "We will have to resort to a temporary restructuring of classes."

"What kind of restructuring?" Layla asked quietly, her heart hitting her ribs in slow, steady thumps. She knew the answer, could read it in Ella's eyes. In a private school, where parents paid big dollars for their children's education, they had more say than in a public school, and apparently the masses had spoken.

"Considering the tremendous…flak… we've received regarding the photo…well, you know how it is. Once a rumor takes hold, it's very difficult to counteract it, and many of our parents are highly reactive. They spend a great deal of money to send their children here...."

Ella continued her long-winded explanation as Layla left her body and floated above the scene, watching herself stare politely at her boss, the picture of composure, while inside she was screaming, "Get on with it already! Tell me that I'm losing Advanced Placement English and taking on Life Skills. Just spit it out!"

"And for that reason..." Ella let out a sigh that made her shoulders sink "...I have no choice but to give Melinda Advanced Placement English and you will take over Life Skills for the next semester."

Layla wasn't fooled. She'd have the position for much longer than one semester. Life Skills—a glorified term for gonzo math and reading for those kids who could buy their way into the school, but didn't give two hoots about grades or learning, despite their parents' desire to make them industrial leaders. Oh, yes, she'd be at the helm until the next new teacher was hired, or another staff member made a misstep—serious enough to alarm parents but not serious enough to be fired. She could have this gig for years and years the way the budget was looking.

"I understand," she said, ever professional. "And I'll quit before I go back to Life Skills."

CHAPTER THREE

THE WORDS STARTLED HER as much as they did Ella.

What had she just said? Why had she said it?

Because she had truly and passionately hated teaching Life Skills during her first year at Manzanita before being moved to Advanced English when Melinda hired on. Life Skills was the baptism by fire at Manzanita, and being a starry-eyed neophyte, she'd felt guilty for not being able to inspire the lazy, entitled kids that populated the class. A teacher taught. But teaching the arrogantly unmotivated was not her cup of tea, and apparently it wasn't Melinda's, either.

"Don't be silly," Ella sputtered. "You were excellent teaching that class. I have a copy of the most recent syllabus," she said, pushing a folder across the table toward Layla. "You can also access it online. Melinda will answer any questions you have."

Layla was certain that Melinda would be delighted to answer *all* her questions.

"I know you will return the favor," the principal added.

"This is not the solution," Layla said adamantly. "These parents are wrong. One misrepresented incident doesn't make me incapable of teaching as I've always taught."

"It's the most logical solution," Ella insisted, nudging the folder closer to her. "Many of the concerned parents have children in your advanced classes. Besides—" she tapped her pencil on the folder "—Melinda just received her master's degree in English, which makes her more qualified."

On paper. "I have every intention of getting my master's," Layla said, focusing on the part of the issue that didn't involve parents. "But I just spent the last two years revamping my English classes, which took up any time I might have used for university courses." Class planning, prep and grading had barely left her any time for a social life, much less continued education. "And," she added, "I won a state merit award for those revamped classes last year." Which Melinda hadn't. That had to eat at her.

Her boss's expression remained impassive. No, it remained stonily stubborn, so Layla gave in to desperation and allowed herself to beg. "Please do not take these classes away from me."

Ella stared at her for a long moment, the end of her pencil making a slow tap, tap, tap on the desk. Finally, she let out a long sigh. "Let's meet tomorrow, after we've both had some time to evaluate the situation." She drew in a long breath through her nose, then opened her calendar. "Say, nine o'clock?"

"Nine o'clock will be fine," Layla said, relief coursing through her at the possible stay of execution. She'd be there at nine, after a good twenty-three hours of figuring out how to save herself. She'd probably look like hell from lack of sleep, since unfinished business invariably gave her insomnia, but she'd be there, and somehow she'd convince Ella to allow her to keep her classes.

USUALLY, JUSTIN WENT TO the catering kitchen in the evenings after Patty had prepped during the day, and worked on his cakes alone. Just him and the music. No interruptions.

He had a lot to do, especially with Patty about to take sick leave, but tonight, the tenth anniversary of signing away parental rights to his then unborn son, he stayed home. Turned on a basketball game and started drinking. Alone. Never a good thing to do, but right now it seemed appropriate.

The first few anniversaries had passed practically unnoticed. Yes, he had a child out there somewhere, one he'd been totally unprepared to care for at the age of eighteen. When his girlfriend, Rachel, had opted for adoption, it had seemed a godsend. No child support. No confessing to his sisters what he'd done. The child was better off with parents who were married and had resources to provide for it. Problem solved.

And if every now and again, in the early hours, he found himself dwelling on the matter, he shoved it out of his mind. A strategy that had worked fairly well until his niece, Rosemary, had been born.

From the moment he'd first felt her warm little body snuggle against his shoulder, watched her mouth form a tiny O as she yawned, he'd been overwhelmed with protective instincts he hadn't even known he possessed. Who would have thought that a baby could make a guy feel like that?

But the kicker was the lost baby, the miscarriage his sister, Reggie, had suffered a little less than a year ago, when she'd been four and a half months pregnant. It had devastated both her and her husband, Tom, to the point that they'd talked of having only the one child because they didn't want to risk another loss. They eventually decided, though, to try one more time and so far, so good, but

Justin was still on edge. He never wanted to see his sister go through that again. He never wanted to go through it again vicariously.

From that point on, denial lost its effectiveness. Kids were not something one signed away and forgot about.

Even if he tamped the thoughts down deep, as deep as he could possibly get them, they slowly but surely worked their way to the surface. He began to notice babies everywhere. And kids. Especially kids about the same age that his son would be.

Justin was a father. Somewhere in the world he had a child. A kid who needed to be protected and loved, as Rosemary needed to be protected and loved.

And he hadn't done that.

It ate at him. Maybe it had always eaten at him in ways he refused to acknowledge.

Last year on the ninth anniversary of the day he'd signed his child away—four months after Rosemary's birth and before Reggie had acknowledged her second pregnancy—he'd sat down in front of the

TV to have a single beer and ended up drinking himself into oblivion.

He planned to repeat the performance tonight. Kind of a yearly ritual, like a birthday party, which worked, since he didn't know when his child had been born. Rachel was sent across the country by her wealthy parents shortly after they'd discovered she was pregnant, and he'd never received word. All he knew was that he had a son, information Rachel had given him after her first ultrasound.

He was on his third beer, blindly watching the game and thinking that whiskey would work faster, when the doorbell rang.

Layla. She'd stopped by the kitchen earlier that afternoon to pick up her overnight bag, which was still here at his apartment. Eden had given her directions and sent her over, then called to warn him.

He appreciated that, because now all the scattered gym socks were in the hamper and he wasn't too deeply into a bottle. That would wait until after she left.

But truth be told, he was on his way to a pretty good buzz. Maybe Layla wouldn't notice.

LAYLA STOOD NERVOUSLY on the concrete outside Justin's second-story condo, hugging her coat closer to her body as protection against the stiff breeze. Why was she so agitated? Not a clue.

Liar. She was tense because Justin made her that way. She never knew what he was going to do, and she hated unpredictability. The door swung open and there he was, barefoot, dressed in washed-out jeans and a plain white T-shirt. His dark blond hair was out of control as always. She wondered if he still cut it himself.

"Layla. What a surprise."

"I bet it is, what with you having my overnight bag and Eden calling to warn you that I was on my way."

He smiled, that cocky Justin smile, but he wasn't looking so cocky with the blackish-yellow circle under his eye. Plus, it was pretty obvious that he'd been drinking. She could smell it on him.

"Would you get it for me, please?" Because all she wanted to do was to get out of here. She'd seen Justin drunk before. He and Derek and Eric had whooped it up a time or two when their parents were gone. Her parents, of course, thought large house-wrecking parties were a rite of passage, and other than making the twins clean up and pay for any damage, turned a blind eye. Stupid, stupid outlook.

"Yeah, sure. You want to come in for a sec?"

"I, uh…no." She gave her head a shake. She did not care to step into the lair.

He shrugged and walked away, holding a beer bottle by the neck. A few seconds later he was back with her small black case in his hand—a gift from Robert. She'd have to donate the bag to charity once she unpacked her clothes.

He held it out and Layla gingerly took it from him, noting that Justin had really nice hands—long, strong fingers that should have been used to make music. She'd forgotten about that—how she'd once told him he should be a musician.

He'd laughed at her, since she'd been so disdainful of her parents' obsession with all things Clapton. She'd been thinking of the violin or the piano, but had left in a huff before explaining matters to him. Justin Tremont playing a piano. Right.

She studied him warily. "I, uh, wanted to thank you for bringing me home Saturday night. And…I hope your eye is all right."

"It's feeling better."

She drew in an audible breath. "Yes. Well. Sorry about that. I can see that you've been taking something for the pain."

"My favorite painkiller." He lifted the bottle of Black Butte Porter he held in his right hand, and Layla suppressed a grimace. Dark beer. *Uck.*

"How many have you had?"

"A few. The game's on and you know how it is with guys, beer and games."

"You sit home alone, drink beer and watch sports?"

"The hookers should be arriving any minute."

"Don't start, Justin. We're not fourteen anymore." She met his eyes. "Well, I'm not, anyway."

"You wouldn't have known that from the other night."

She didn't have an answer for that one, but she did have another question. "Uh… what all did I tell you? After you brought me home?"

"You really want to know?"

"I wouldn't be asking otherwise."

"Let's see…that bastard is sleeping with your trollop of a coworker." He shrugged. "That about sums it up."

Did she see pity in his eyes? Dear heavens, she hoped not, because she would not tolerate pity from Justin. "That's all?"

"For the most part. I'm sorry about what happened."

"I'm sorry about parts of it," Layla said, thinking it was a sad day when she was confessing her troubles to Justin, even if he was rather intimately involved. But the situation was gnawing at her.

"What part?"

She looked up at him, meeting those

rather amazing green eyes. Such a waste. He'd grown from an obnoxious skinny kid into a very striking guy. "The part where it affects my job."

"Because of the trollop?" His shoulders were hunched against the brisk breeze that was blowing past him into his condo, and Layla heard the furnace kick on. Yet he stood in the open doorway, waiting for her response instead of sending her off and stepping back into his warm house.

"Yes, because of the trollop. I…" Layla gave an impatient, dismissive gesture. "It's a long story."

"I have time."

She blinked at his unexpected response. His expression remained serious. No smirk. Nothing. She narrowed her eyes slightly, gauging him. Something about this didn't seem right.

Was it possible that he didn't want to drink and watch the game alone? Well, if he was soliciting her company, then he must truly be desperate for companionship.

The hookers must have canceled.

Justin stepped back before she answered one way or the other, and gestured for her to come inside. Layla fought with herself briefly, then shrugged and walked into his front room, trying not to be too obvious as she took a quick inventory.

It was a guy place. Leather furniture, a giant TV where the Celtics were playing the Bulls with the sound muted. There was a pile of running shoes against the wall next to the front door and a cardboard box filled with women's clothing. A black, lacy bit of lingerie was tossed carelessly on top. Oh, criminy. Was the woman, whoever she was, going to come home while Layla was here?

No. This looked more like a moving-out box. A toothbrush was jammed into one corner. No wonder Justin was looking for company. He probably wouldn't mind a bit of sympathy, too.

"Have a seat," he said as he shut the door and led the way across the room to the U-shaped sectional. Chalk-colored leather. Surprisingly tasteful, with a dark oak coffee table, strewn with cookbooks and sports magazines, nestled in the center of the U. Two empty beer bottles stood side by side at one end.

Layla perched on the edge of the sectional, impressed with how comfortable it was, and Justin settled a few feet away.

"So let's hear this long story."

"How drunk are you?" she asked.

He shrugged. "Not very, but if you don't want me to remember, I won't."

He gave her that roguish Justin grin she was so familiar with, and Layla smiled in spite of herself. But the smile faded as she said, "One of the students at the lake took a photo of me throwing up in the bush and posted it on Facebook. Many concerned parents phoned in, and ultimately my principal decided to demote me to Life Skills and give Melinda my advanced English classes."

"Who's Melinda?" he asked. Layla raised her eyebrows significantly and he formed a silent "oh." "The trollop?"

"The same."

"Life Skills is bad?"

"Life Skills is a class for the kids whose

parents can pay the steep Manzanita tuition, but who don't perform at the desired level."

"They have learning disabilities?" Justin asked with a slight frown.

"No. This has nothing to do with ability and everything to do with attitude. Students who *can't* achieve but want to learn are in special tutorial classes. This class is for kids who *won't* achieve. They are entitled and lazy, and the teacher's job is to try to motivate them when they know they're safe in their parents' protection no matter what they do."

"Why aren't they just kicked out of the school?"

"Are you kidding? In this economy?" Layla rubbed her thumb and first two fingers together. "Money…"

Justin leaned back against the cushions, obviously more comfortable with the conversation than she was, and studied his beer for a moment.

"I taught this class before," Layla continued darkly. "My first year. It was rugged. I hated it."

And she'd never told anyone that before. Maybe she felt safe because he was drinking. Maybe she just needed to tell someone the sad truth—that she was in some ways a rotten teacher. "I meet with the principal tomorrow and we'll hash this out."

Hopefully, she'd be able to convince Ella that it would be disruptive to the students to change teachers nine weeks before the school year ended. Then she would convince her boss that the parents would forget about the unfortunate incident by the time the long summer break was over.

"What if she doesn't budge?"

Layla's throat closed slightly. "I...think I'd quit."

"And then what?"

She gave a quick shrug. "I'd probably work for Sam until I get another teaching job." She looked him in the eye before saying adamantly, "I'm not going to back down."

"I don't blame you. Life is too short to do something you hate for very long."

Layla stared at him for a moment. As a teen, Justin had always done as he damned well pleased, and she'd often told herself that he was wrong to do so. That it was immature to follow the heart instead of the head. But honestly? She hadn't been all that happy following her head, and life *was* short.

"What does Sam do now?" Justin asked. "Does she still have the bead store?"

"No. She has a small clothing and gift boutique that she started last year after the bead shop tanked. Sunshine of Your Love."

Justin smiled. "No offense, but it sounds like a head shop."

"It's worse than that. She, uh…" Layla raised her eyebrows meaningfully. "Sunshine of your *love*…"

"Sex toys?" Justin asked, unable to keep the delight out of his voice.

"Gifts for lovers to share," Layla said primly. "Along with funky clothing, lingerie and regular items. Balloon bouquets, greeting cards."

"I'd love to see the balloons."

"No you wouldn't."

"Your family is nuts, Layla."

"I know."

"I mean that in a good way."

"What kind of good way? What could possibly be good about shirking responsibility?"

"How is it irresponsible to run a business?"

"If you saw how Sam did it, you'd understand." The bead business had sunk slowly but surely as her sister bought stock and put off paying for it. But Sam hadn't had much business traffic, either. Sunshine was doing much, much better. Apparently more people wanted to invest in their love life than in jewelry making.

Layla let her head fall back against the buttery-soft leather sofa cushions, but resisted the urge to close her eyes and luxuriate for a moment. None of her furniture was this good. She'd bought cheap stuff, saving her money for more important things, like her retirement fund.

This seemed so wrong. She'd formulated a plan, made sacrifices to stick to it, and everything was supposed to turn out all right. The end. She wasn't supposed to be demoted back to Life Skills. Or have to go work for her sister, who couldn't afford to pay her.

Justin got up and went into the kitchen on the other side of the breakfast island and opened the fridge. "Sure you don't want one?" he asked. Layla shook her head and he pulled out a single beer.

"Do you always drink alone?"

"I'm trying hard not to," he pointed out.

Layla scowled at his purposeful misinterpretation. "Did your girlfriend move out?"

Justin glanced over at the box. "Very astute, Watson."

"It was the toothbrush." And it explained why he was drinking.

"But, no, I don't usually drink alone and it isn't because of Cindy." Spoken like a man.

"Why today? Special occasion?" To Layla's surprise, there was a fleeting touch of bitterness in his answering smile. There, then gone.

"In a manner of speaking." He held the unopened bottle loosely, contemplating it for a moment. "An anniversary of sorts."

"I see." But she obviously didn't. And she'd never known Justin to be anything close to morose. It bothered her. "What kind of anniversary?"

He shrugged, and she could see he wasn't about to give her a straight answer. Instead, he cocked his head, and the old Justin was back. The one she knew and could deal with. "What do you think about me, Layla?"

"Can I use long words? Or shall we stick with monosyllabic?"

"Your choice."

"I think you've never had boundaries. You live life in a free-form way. I don't believe you give a hoot for consequences. And because of that, sometimes you have to drink alone."

"You think I'm irresponsible?"

Layla sighed. "Not exactly. I'm saying that in some aspects of your life you are more haphazard than in others."

He studied her intently for a moment

before saying, "Which aspects?" For some reason he needed her to spell it out. Fine. She'd spell.

"Well, judging from what went on in high school, you tend to be mercurial in your personal relationships." She gestured toward the box. "How many of those have you had in your life?"

"A few," he admitted.

"But on the other hand, you're part of a successful business." She shifted her head on the leather sofa cushion to look at him. "So who am I to judge?" *And what could you possibly care about my thoughts after all these years?*

She got to her feet. It seemed like a good time to go. In fact, suddenly she felt as if she couldn't get out of there fast enough. Something was off here…something that didn't feel like it used to, and it was making her patently uncomfortable. Why was Justin asking her opinion of him? And in such a deeply serious way. And why was he suddenly looking like an attractive guy instead of her archrival?

"I need to get back home," she said lamely. "I have…stuff to do." More lameness.

"Do you make a spreadsheet or something for that?" he asked mildly. Layla didn't bother answering. She picked up the case and Justin walked with her to the door. When they got there, he put his hand on the knob as if he was going to open it for her, then said, "We've been through a lot, you and I."

"Meaning you made my life miserable when I was a kid? Yes."

"If you hadn't been so easy to mess with, so…reactive…"

"Blaming the victim, Justin?" she asked softly.

"You were never a victim. You gave as good as you got." He touched his bruised cheekbone.

Funny, but she didn't remember it that way. Maybe she'd tried, but… "I was never in your league, Justin, so it wasn't a fair contest."

He frowned a little, his expression dis-

tant, as if calling up a long lost memory—
something that involved her, no doubt.

"No. You held your own."

Never argue with the intoxicated—even
the slightly intoxicated. She couldn't judge
how drunk he was. A little? A lot?

Layla smiled tightly and reached for the
doorknob. Before she could turn it, Justin
put his hand over hers, startling her. When
her eyes flashed up at his, he slowly and
deliberately lowered his head until their
lips met. And heaven help her, she opened
her mouth to his. Instinctively. Because
that was what one did when kissed.

She could taste the beer on his tongue,
felt an unexpected flash of heat shoot
through her. Then she put both hands on
his chest and pushed him back.

"You owe me an apology, Justin."

He let out a soft exhalation. "I don't
agree, but I'll tell you what. Do you want
to work for your sister? If you do end up
quitting tomorrow."

"I…no." She wasn't going to argue that
she wasn't planning to quit. Justin wasn't
listening.

"Work for me then."

"Oh, yes," she said, rolling her eyes. "That would be so much better." He was going off his rocker or he was much, much drunker than he looked. That was the only explanation for the kiss, the job offer. There was no explanation for her own response, except for the surprise and novelty factor. That was it. She didn't have enough spontaneity in her life. Everything was always planned to the T. She'd have to do something about that—in a way that didn't involve Justin.

"It'd be a perfect solution if worse came to worst. I need temporary help. Patty, my assistant, will be out for surgery next week. She's supposed to be gone for six weeks, but if she knows I have another assistant, I bet she'll be back in four."

It figured that he had an angle. "I—"

"I'm not asking you to bake. I'm asking you to follow directions. In return, you'll get a handsome paycheck and something new on your résumé while you look for that perfect next job. Plus I can probably give you more hours than Sam."

What was Layla dealing with? Pity? Lust? Rebound effect? The thought of Justin rebounding with her was ludicrous. "No," she said, taking refuge in extreme politeness. "But thanks for the offer."

"Why not come work for me?"

She lifted one edge of her mouth in a gently smirking half smile. "Because you're drunk and will regret making this offer in the morning. A condition I'm certain you're used to, but this time I'm going to save you from yourself."

She reached up to lightly touch his stubble-roughened cheek, just to show that she wasn't the least affected by his kiss. "But thanks for the offer, Justin. I'll see you around."

He smiled at what was obviously a lie, since she was going to take great efforts not to see him, and stepped back. "Yeah, Layla. Sounds good." He hoisted the bottle in a salute.

She was barely outside the door—retreating, as she always did after a confrontation with Justin— when what he'd said sank in: she'd given as good as she'd got.

Had she?

Maybe not, but it was never too late to set matters straight. She turned and knocked. Justin opened the door, a questioning expression on his face that froze there when she pulled his head down and kissed him.

"What was that for?" he said when she released him.

"That was for every time I've taken the high road and didn't respond in kind to all the stuff you and Derek and Eric did to me."

He rubbed his thumb over his lower lip. "I like the way you retaliate."

"Do you?"

"Yeah."

"Well…good." With that Layla spun around and walked down the steps. It did feel good to retaliate, and she wasn't going to think about the part where kissing Justin was a turn-on.

CHAPTER FOUR

AFTER HOURS OF TOSSING sleeplessly, Layla finally drifted off, only to wake suddenly to the disturbing thought that everything she knew, everything she'd believed in and had built on, was wrong.

Why else would she be in this position after trying so hard to do everything right?

She lay in bed staring at the ceiling instead of leaping into action as usual, but the renegade thoughts didn't evaporate. They continued playing in her head as she got out of bed and showered, brushed her teeth, put on her makeup. As she prepared for her meeting with Ella.

Predictable. By the book. Rule follower. That was her. She wasn't a wimp, but she did tend to avoid controversy. Someone in her family had to. And that was probably what Ella was banking on. She figured Layla would give in, take the transfer to Life Skills out of a sense of professionalism. What her boss didn't know was that, when push came to shove, Layla had a backbone.

That trollop was not getting her advanced class without a fight.

Kissing Justin seemed to have jarred something loose in her brain. She felt positively rebellious, and realized with a start that perhaps there was more Taylor in her than she'd realized. Perhaps she wasn't the image of stick-in-the-mud Grandmother Bonnie.

Maybe she wasn't going to take it anymore—not even to keep her job.

Layla was loading the coffee filter with fresh grounds when she heard the distinctive squeak of her front steps. Doorbell ditchers and surprise visitors never had much luck at Layla's house because of that squeak.

Who on earth would be here at this time of the morning?

Justin again? Her heart did a small pitter-pat.

Robert.

He was halfway down the steps when she opened the door and nearly tripped over the box he'd left there.

"Hey!"

His head jerked around, his guilty gaze meeting hers. "Layla," he said. "I didn't want to wake you."

"You certainly haven't wasted time cutting all ties," she said with clenched teeth. He'd probably counted on her being asleep. Coward.

The coward straightened up, shoved his hands into his overcoat pockets, and she felt a deep need to make him suffer. "Will you carry it inside for me?"

"Yeah, sure." He eyed her cautiously as he headed back up the steps and hefted the box she could have picked up herself, trailing snow behind him as he walked into the house.

"On the coffee table there."

"It's heavy. There're a lot of books in it." Books she'd shared with him, though she suspected he hadn't read any of them, since he'd put her off whenever she tried to discuss them.

"It's a sturdy table." Layla swung the door shut and stood in front of it, barring escape—for a few minutes, anyway. Less than a week ago she'd fancied herself in love with this snake. "How long have you been sleeping with Melinda?"

"Layla…there's nothing to gain by dissecting this situation."

"Closure, Robert. I need closure." He shifted his weight uncomfortably. "Shortly after the Christmas party, I'm guessing."

He shrugged, giving her the answer she needed through omission. Two months. Two months she'd been sleeping with him while he'd been sleeping with Melinda. It made her feel sick.

"Did she initially call you or…?"

Robert straightened his back, rolled his shoulders slightly. "I called her."

"Why?" Layla's lips were dry, but she didn't moisten them, didn't want to give one sign of the pain coursing through her. Not pain at losing Robert, but pain at being such a trusting fool.

"She was interesting."

"And I wasn't?"

"I didn't say that, Layla." He focused on a spot somewhere over her left shoulder. "But she doesn't have so many…parameters."

Layla frowned. Forced herself not to become defensive, because that wouldn't help her obtain her objective. "Parameters."

"Rules. Regulations."

Robert was an anal engineer, and he was put off by her parameters? She'd thought he'd lived for parameters, and she said so.

He took a couple nervous paces over to the nearest basket wicker chair, his hands still shoved deep into his pockets. "But not in every aspect of life. Damn it, Layla, you have many fine qualities."

Fine qualities? She clenched her fists. It sounded as if she were a prize heifer.

"But they're overshadowed by your…" He pulled a hand out of his pocket and gestured in a way that expressed frustration. "Being such a tight ass."

Despite her anger, Layla felt a wash of old insecurities sweep over her. Insecurities from her adolescent years that she was old enough to have moved past, but somehow hadn't. Not totally, anyway.

"In all arenas?" she asked softly.

"The sex was good," he said.

"Thank you for that."

"But it could have been better…if you had been able to cut loose." He may as well have slapped her. The-man-is-always-on-the-top Robert wanted her to cut loose. She had done that quite nicely in the parking lot at Lake Tahoe. His nose was still red and slightly swollen.

"That works both ways," she said without missing a beat, but inwardly she was curling up, dying. She'd never been all that secure in the personal relationship area, and now Robert was standing there, confirming her fears. "Why the hell didn't you just break up with me?" He didn't answer, and Layla had a sudden flash of insight. "You liked the danger."

"No…" He made another gesture, negating her theory, but his face said it all. Robert was so easy to read—good thing, too, or she would still be with him. Clueless. Playing the chump.

"Well," she said, wishing she hadn't invited him in, but thankful for hearing his interpretation of the truth. "Thank you for bringing my stuff back. I wish you and Melinda every happiness." She opened the door and all but pushed him outside.

A second later, after closing the door with a quiet, definite click instead of slamming it as she wanted to, she heard the distinctive creak, creak, creak.

Robert creaking out of her life, and all she felt was cold, mind-numbing anger.

JUSTIN WOKE WITH THE HEADACHE he deserved.

After Layla had left last night, he'd settled back on the sofa with his beer and started thinking and drinking instead of watching the game, which remained on mute. He reflected on how he'd hid from thoughts of his kid over the years. Protected himself. Refused to allow the child to be real. Because then he'd have to deal with feelings he didn't know how to categorize or manage.

Would he have been able to remain in denial if Reggie hadn't made him an uncle to the world's cutest baby girl? He didn't know. It was very possible that the worry, the concern and the guilt would have come anyway.

A few years back he'd suddenly realized that his son was about to start first grade. The thought had startled him. Hell, Justin could remember starting first grade himself, going to school hanging on to Reggie's hand. But he'd been able to tamp down the feelings, excuse himself from the memories, step back into denial.

Tell himself this was all for the best.

It was getting harder to do that—mainly because he had questions that wouldn't go away. Was his kid all right? Were the child's parents taking good care of him? Did they love him the way Reggie and Tom loved Rosemary?

And then he'd tell himself that his kid

was fine. He was the one with the problem, he was the one who'd signed the papers for a closed adoption, thus ensuring he'd never be able to get answers to any questions he might have, and he'd simply have to carry on.

What more could he do?

Finish drinking his six-pack and toss in a shot of Jack for good measure.

Cindy had come and gone while he was sleeping, taking her box of stuff and leaving her key on the coffee table. So much for goodbyes. Justin wasn't much for goodbyes, anyway—although he should be with the practice he'd had lately.

He showered, letting the spray beat on his back until the water started to grow cold. Had Layla felt this rough after her binge the other night?

Layla.

He smacked a hand on top of his wet hair, the water channeling through his fingers and over his face. He'd kissed Layla. Two or three beers in, when she'd stopped by to get her bag.

And not only had he kissed her, he'd offered her a job?

The water was getting really cold, but still Justin stood under it, torturing himself as the memories continued to surface. He'd kissed Layla. How stupid could he get?

He cranked off the shower control. He'd been stupid because she'd caught him in a weak moment. A time when his guard was down and he'd needed...human contact. Something. And there she'd been.

He grabbed a towel, sniffed it to make sure it was relatively clean. He really had to get a housekeeper or something. The towel passed muster and he rubbed it over his head.

So he'd kissed her. No big deal. She'd demanded an apology, too.

Very Layla.

And then she'd left, come back and kissed him. With a vengeance.

Not at all like Layla.

That could quite possibly represent a big deal. He shook his head as he toweled off.

Or not.

Regardless, he did owe her an apology...and he also needed to withdraw that job offer.

Justin skipped breakfast, buying a cup of coffee on the way to the kitchen, and pulled into the front lot of Tremont Catering a few minutes later than scheduled.

Eden was already at the stove when he walked in through the reception area. Reggie, who was once again pregnant and ultracareful after losing the last child, wasn't supposed to arrive until after noon, due to a doctor's appointment, leaving them short a cook. It was going to be rough with both Reggie and Patty out.

"You're hungover," Eden said.

"Maybe a little," he agreed, taking a look at the calendar. The kitchen was slow during late March, just prior to wedding season, so maybe they would be all right. But he still had a steady stream of cake orders for various occasions. Eden was awful with icing, so she wasn't getting near the stuff. Besides, she had a job and a half to do, plus planning her own small May wedding to Nick Duncan, the detective who'd mistakenly thought Tremont Catering was involved in money laundering. He'd also believed his job was the center of his world after losing his wife, but Eden had taught him a thing or two.

"Because of Cindy?"

"Maybe," he said, hoping she'd drop the matter.

"Why do you only date people that are obviously wrong for you?" his sister asked, lowering her spoon to her side.

"Self-preservation," Justin replied easily.

"From what?"

"Look," he said patiently, "I know that people engaged to be married, such as yourself, want everyone else to be as happy as they are, but some of us are thrilled to be single. I can leave my socks wherever I want, eat what I want, go to bed when I want—"

"Are you talking about having a mother?"

"I'm talking about being single and liking it. Living life the way I want to. And I date women I enjoy. Who enjoy me. We're just not the committing type."

"Cindy was."

"How do you know?"

"We talked."

"Saints preserve us," Justin muttered, heading into his pastry room. Eden, of course, followed him, to finish a conversation he didn't want to finish. He took her by the shoulders, turned her around and gave her a gentle push toward the door.

"You are going to live out your years a lonely man," she called before the door shut.

Yes, he probably was, because he couldn't let his relationships move past a certain point.

He and Cindy had hit that point.

And he shouldn't have kissed Layla.

LAYLA USUALLY WALKED INTO the school with a sense of purpose, rapidly ticking off items on a mental agenda, but today she had only one item on her list—take back her English classes. Before the disastrous evening at the lake, she'd been a huge proponent of the stiff upper lip.

Today she was operating on more of a what-the-hell Taylor attitude and it felt good. Empowering.

Seeing Melinda's little blue sports car parked close to the rear entrance only increased her resolve. She was *not* going to be in a position where she had to listen to Melinda brag about the class that Layla had created, and she would never again suffer the sleepless nights and chronic headaches induced by Life Skills. Okay, so she was a horrible person and teacher. She wouldn't do it.

Francine, the school secretary, pointed at Ella's half-open office door as soon as Layla walked in. Layla smiled as if this was just an everyday kind of meeting, and Francine smiled back. Weakly. They weren't fooling one another. This was not an ordinary meeting.

The principal sat behind her broad oak desk, hands folded in front of her, her expression cool to the point of frigid, causing Layla's steps to slow as she entered the room. She'd never seen her boss this way and it was more than a little unnerving.

"Good morning," she said in a voice that sounded confident and professional and just a wee bit brittle, as she came to stand in front of the desk. "Please sit down."

Layla sat, her back perfectly straight, taking slow, calming breaths. "Thank you," she murmured.

"Have you made a decision?" Ella asked point-blank. For a moment the blunt question hung there as Layla formed her answer. She'd expected more preliminaries.

"I want to continue in English," she said. Her fingers twisted the lowest button on her cardigan and she abruptly stopped the movement.

"That is not an option." It was a proclamation.

"No?"

Ella gave her silvery head one firm shake. "No."

"Then why the meeting?" Layla asked,

acting on instinct and sounding far less deferential than usual. "And why should I lose a class I've built from the ground up because of one unfortunate incident?"

"The parents, Layla," Ella reminded her in a tone of exaggerated patience.

Yes, the parents had something to do with it. Private schools were just that—private entities. She could be tossed out on her ear on a whim. High price to pay for the privilege of teaching a more exclusive group of students. However, the decision was based on more than parental pressure. Layla was certain of it.

"It's Melinda," she said in a low voice.

"Melinda?" Ella rested her forearms on the desk with a mystified scowl.

"Has she ever spoken to you about taking over my classes?"

"Not recently." Perhaps not, but Melinda was excellent at planting seeds. She couldn't have foreseen the fallout from the photo, but she would have set the stage to get what she wanted, just in case Layla had reason to leave the school.

"You don't believe *she* posted the photo?" Ella asked, sounding shocked.

"I don't know about that." To Layla it wasn't out of the realm of possibility. "But I wouldn't put it past her to have stirred up the parents over this issue. She's competitive—" *i.e., a sweet-faced barracuda* "—and willing to take advantage of a situation."

The shocked look remained on Ella's face, a testimony to Melinda's abilities in subterfuge and ass-kissing. "She's an excellent teacher. The students love her."

"True." Layla hated to admit it, but the kids did love her. "But she's wanted my classes since she got here."

"This sounds very paranoid, Layla."

It did. But she wasn't paranoid. She was closer to the situation than Ella and had a few more facts....

"Will you take the transfer to Life Skills?" the principal asked.

"No," she said firmly.

"Layla…"

"Melinda is sleeping with my boyfriend." She blurted out the words, even though she hadn't intended to say them at all. But what the hell? She was beginning to hear the fat lady sing. "She sneaked around with Robert and now she's trying to steal my classes. No. I will not go to Life Skills."

Ella's expression was now one of extreme distaste. Because of Layla blurting out the truth about her private life? Or because Melinda's actions had been sleazy and unforgivable?

"That is a private matter," the older woman decreed, answering the question. "Will you take the transfer?"

Layla stood, gathering the strap of her purse in both hands. "I will not go to Life Skills."

"In that case, after the close of this school term, we no longer need your services."

Layla heard the words as if through a cotton wool filter. She tilted her head, then gave it a tiny shake. "I'm fired?"

"Your contract will not be renewed next semester."

"I'm fired."

"You will not be renewed after you finish out this semester."

She was so damned glad she hadn't wimped out and taken the transfer yesterday, only to have this happen. At least now she had some pride left. Not much, but enough to allow her to pack and leave the building with her head held high.

She'd wait until she got home to collapse into a heap of insecurity and quite possibly tears.

She met Ella's pale gaze. "I don't think I will finish out the semester." Down the hall from smug, smirking Melinda, who would know that Layla had been sacked. She'd have won. Yay!

"You'll break your contract?"

"I'll take my sick days." There were nine weeks of classes left after spring hiatus. She'd have two days to spare.

"You aren't sick."

"Oh, no. I am. This situation is making me sick. I'm being railroaded under the most ridiculous circumstances."

Ella's nostrils flared, but before she could speak, Layla said, "I'll just go pack up my room." She turned smartly and started toward the door, maintaining her composure only because she was in absolute shock.

"No."

The curt response stopped her dead. She turned back. "Excuse me?"

"You will not use your sick days and you will not be allowed back into a classroom here at Manzanita Prep. I'm sorry, but your services are no longer required, effective immediately, and you'll have to leave the building. Walter will escort you out."

Walter will what? Layla felt her throat closing. "I don't understand."

Ella held out her hand. "Please give me your keys."

Layla slowly shook her head, not fully grasping what was happening. She couldn't get her belongings?

"You'll get all your personal things back," Ella assured her.

"But my lesson plans, the materials I've developed...I did that on my own time.

Those are *mine*." Layla spoke from between clenched teeth.

"Your personal belongings will be returned to you in short order," Ella replied. "It would be illegal for us to keep them."

Layla couldn't stop the sneer from forming on her face. "And you wouldn't want to do anything illegal. But you will toss me neatly under the bus." She took her keys out of her jacket pocket and slapped them down on the table. "I want everything. All the lessons plans, the units, everything. Those are mine."

And she wasn't going to get them— at least not until every page was photocopied. She could see it in Ella's face. The principal wouldn't want to lose the materials that had won Layla the state merit award for excellence. She would want to hand them off to Melinda or one of her other teachers.

Layla turned on her heel and headed for the door, only to run straight into Walter's six-foot-two-inch frame. She looked up at the security man's stern face as he took hold of her arm.

He didn't exactly frog-march her out of the office, but he wouldn't loosen his hold. Layla was "escorted" down the hall and out the door into the rear parking lot. Only then did his expression soften.

"Sorry about that," he muttered.

"Why did she do this?" Layla asked, tears starting to sting her eyes now that reaction was setting in and she was far enough away from the Wicked Witch of the West not to lose face.

Walter's mouth flattened and he looked slightly embarrassed at his role in the matter. She'd always gotten along well with him. "Common practice so dismissed employees don't have the opportunity to vandalize anything in anger."

"I understand," Layla said automatically. But she didn't. She didn't understand any of this. Last Friday she'd been a happy teacher about to go on vacation. Now she was an unhappy teacher without a job.

All because of…way too many things that seemed to align at one time. A perfect cosmic junction of bad luck, and Layla had been smack in the center of it.

The tears that had built up started to fall, streaming down her cheek as she walked to her car, head down. She refused to wipe them away in case Ella or Melinda or anyone else was watching from a window. And the crazy thing was they were more tears of anger than anything else. Layla felt steamrolled. Misused.

And mad as hell about it.

The depression phase would no doubt follow the anger, but right now she was hanging on to her outrage, because it helped numb any other emotions that might come crashing down on her.

She got into the car and slammed the door before staring blankly out the window. So where did she go now?

Home? Sam's place?

She swallowed the giant lump in her throat and started the engine, hoping she could get out of the parking lot without giving in to the very strong urge to smash her car straight into Melinda's little blue Mitsubishi Eclipse.

Maybe Melinda hadn't engineered this, but she was benefiting, and she'd been screwing Layla's boyfriend at night and smiling at Layla during the day.

JUSTIN'S HEADACHE HAD abated after a couple hours of work, so he had no excuse for snapping at Eden when she asked why he'd taken another cake order when he was already swamped. Wearily, she made a face and headed out of his room, obviously writing his bad mood off to the hangover.

He braced his hands on the table and let his head drop after Eden closed the door with exaggerated care. He'd taken the cake order because he wanted to bury himself in work. Keep from thinking.

Ten years.

His son had made it ten years without him. He'd made it for ten years without knowing anything about his son. And they'd been okay years. No reason he couldn't continue the way he had up until now—except that he couldn't shake the questions, which in turn led to the guilt.

What if his son had needed him and he hadn't been there?

He turned the music up another couple notches and started dropping butter into the mixing bowl. He was, of course, making a birthday cake today. One of dozens he'd made over the past few years, so it shouldn't bother him. He wasn't going to let it bother him. Determined, he set to work.

"You SHOULD HAVE SMACKED her car," Sam said adamantly. "Just nicked the bumper, if nothing else. I think you missed an opportunity."

Layla tried to smile, but couldn't get the job done. She should have gone home. Should have accepted the transfer to Life Skills. Should have simply gone to work every day and put up with Melinda living her—Layla's—life, teaching her classes, sleeping with her boyfriend.

Layla let out a low groan. She was ashamed. Embarrassed.

What had happened to her newly discovered rebel self?

Easy. Rebel Layla had gotten smacked firmly backward and now was whimpering in a corner—or rather, sitting on her sister's purple sofa with an emerald-green afghan pulled over her ugly teacher clothes.

Guess she wouldn't be wearing those again for a while.

"You'll get another job," Sam said as she tossed various items—a necklace, a lipstick, a small pair of needle-nose pliers—into her huge tote bag. Layla could see a Pop-Tart box poking out of the interior. "And until then you can help me. No sweat."

No sweat. Just get another job. Work at a boutique for free, since her sister could barely afford to pay herself.

Layla tugged the afghan closer to her chin.

"Are you sure you even want to be a teacher?" Sam asked suddenly. Layla scowled at her.

"Of course I want to be a teacher. I've always wanted to be a teacher. Why would you ask such a question?"

Sam picked up the tote bag and gave it a slight shake so that everything settled into place with a few clinks and muffled clanks. "Because you've never seemed very happy doing it."

"I'm happy! Or I was happy."

Sam propped a hand on her hip. "What about all those headaches and stomachaches you keep talking about?"

"When you're dealing with adolescents, headaches are a given," Layla said primly.

"Well, I don't get them in my job, so I don't see why you have to get them in yours."

Because I take things more seriously than you do!

Sam set down the bag and came to perch on the edge of the sofa, clasping her hands together in her lap. "I don't quite know how to say this, but...Layla, I don't think you've been happy for a long time."

Layla opened her mouth to protest, to talk about professional gratification and the value of sacrifice—to defend her choices for the past decade and a half—

but Sam cut her off before she got out more than a syllable.

"I know what you're going to say. I know exactly what you're going to say. But stop. Just stop. Okay?"

She seemed to be waiting for a response, so Layla nodded.

"You are on the cusp of something. You got fired for a reason and now you need to explore options—"

"Turn lemons into lemonade?" Layla interjected bitterly.

"Lemonade?" Sam said, wrinkling her nose. "No. You have the chance to investigate other opportunities and you should damned well take it. And maybe go back and clip Melinda's bumper while you're at it."

"I..." *Have no idea what to say.* "What options?"

"Haven't you ever wanted to be something other than a teacher? An astronaut or a cowboy?" Sam held up a hand. "I was being facetious with those choices. But, really. Have you ever thought of trying something else?"

"No."

"Or dating another kind of man?"

"I date stable men."

"Maybe you should try to date fun men. Men who aren't husband material, but who can give you some most excellent experiences without being The One."

"Experiences…"

Sam shrugged. "Yes," she said simply. "More numbers in your equation." She leaned forward and grasped Layla's wrist. "Take advantage of this. Yes, look for a job. But…don't just jump back into your old life, because you may well be there forever. Shop. Experience."

"Eat, love, pray?"

Sam nodded. "If that's what it takes." She glanced at the watch hanging on a chain around her neck. "I have to go if I'm going to open on time. Are you coming?"

"Not today. I have a few things I should do at home." Layla pushed the afghan aside. "But I am going to consider what you said." Because it made sense, which kind of frightened her.

"Good." Sam hoisted the bag into her

shoulder. "You don't want to turn into Grandma Bonnie."

"Whose careful saving habits bankrolled your business. And Eric's business and Derek's fire academy training."

"And who never smiled," Sam said, starting for the door. "Think about that."

Layla did think about that. For the rest of the day. She also fought fear of never being gainfully employed again, and anger at having her lessons stolen. And shame. She fought the shame. How was she going to explain to people about losing her job?

Perhaps she could say she was going back to grad school. This would be the perfect time. For one tiny insane split second she thought about begging Ella for a second chance. That was the old Layla talking. The new wounded-yet-determined-to-grow-stronger Layla told her to shut up. No begging.

She thought about Sam's advice to date a guy just for fun instead of searching for The One. Layla wondered if she could do that. Dating in that way seemed to lack purpose. Why waste time just having fun with someone who was going to disappear from her life? Such as Justin.

Why not?

She could come up with a few pat answers, but the fact remained that Justin stirred something in her, made her believe that there were adventures to be had merely for the experience—something she'd never considered before. Experiences needed to serve a purpose. Be built upon. Be sensible.

That was how she'd lived her life—which was crumbling around her—up until now.

Could it be that, for the first time in recorded history, her sister was more in line with reality than she was? That she honestly did need to discover a life in which she smiled more?

JUSTIN LEFT THE KITCHEN eight hours after arriving. It was one of those rare days when he didn't have to stay late to get everything on his list accomplished. He stood next to his car for a moment and rubbed the tense muscles in the back of his neck.

Did he go home and deal with the nagging anxiety and dark thoughts in the way he was most tempted to—with beer? Give his friend Donovan a shout to see if he wanted to do something? Head on down to Ceol, his favorite Irish pub, to see what was shaking on a Tuesday night?

Really torture himself and drop by Reggie and Tom's place and play with his niece?

He'd go home. He didn't like the way Reggie had been studying him of late, as if trying to figure out what was wrong with him. He'd never kept many secrets from his sisters—serious ones, anyway. The only secret he'd kept was this one, because at what point did he tell? Years had passed, years during which he'd assumed things would get better for him.

He drove to his condo and let himself into his very empty place. This was what he wanted, though. A private space. A retreat. So why did his home feel so uninviting?

Because he lived here alone with his thoughts, which were getting out of hand.

He was on his way to the fridge, to see what he had in the way of nonalcoholic beverages, when someone knocked on the door. A light, almost tentative sound. Probably that kid from the third floor selling cookies or wrapping paper—a one-girl sales machine.

He opened the door and found himself facing Layla.

CHAPTER FIVE

"THIS IS A SURPRISE," he said, standing back in case she wanted to come inside.

One corner of her mouth lifted slightly at his ironic tone. "No doubt. We've seen each other maybe five times in the past five years and three of those have been in the last week."

"Exactly. Did you lose something else?"

She didn't answer immediately, but instead stood studying his face, as if trying to find the answer to some riddle. Or perhaps a clue to what exactly had happened the night before.

"I want to apologize for last night," he said. It seemed the proper thing to say. It might even be the reason she was here, but somehow he didn't think so.

"Then it follows that I should do the same," she said, eyeing him calmly. The breeze lifted her straight dark hair, ruffled her bangs. She pushed away the strands that blew across her face.

"May I come in?" she asked.

"Yeah. Sure." He and Layla were beyond politeness-for-the-sake-of-politeness.

Once he closed the door, she stood without moving, her hands in her pockets.

"Why did you kiss me?"

His heart jumped at the point-blank question. "Damned if I know."

"I guess that makes two of us." She shifted her weight slightly, telling him she was not entirely comfortable, but then, neither was he. "And I don't like things I don't understand." She bit her lip in a considering manner as she continued to study his face. He could not for the life of him come up with a flippant rejoinder.

The foyer where they stood was dimly lit, making the pale leather sofa in the living room shine like a welcoming beacon in the glow of the reading light. Layla kept glancing over at it and finally he said, "You want a beer or something?"

"No…" She looked up at him, her expression more candid and vulnerable than he ever remembered. Usually the force fields were up. "But I wouldn't mind staying for just a minute, if it's all right."

"Have a seat," Justin said, trying to figure out just what the hell was going on, why she was here.

She walked ahead of him to the sofa, hands still in her pockets, then sat down, closing her eyes as she leaned back against the cushion. The tension in her shoulders eased until he sat down next to her, and then they went rigid again. This was the Layla he knew and was comfortable with.

She opened her eyes, turned her head on the cushion to look at him, her dark hair fanning over her shoulder with the movement. And still she didn't say anything.

Wow. Was she in shock? He'd never seen Layla silent for so long. Or maybe he'd never given her a chance to be quiet. He'd always been prodding for reaction.

"Kiss me again."

Now *his* shoulders went tense. "What?"

"I need to know something. Please kiss me."

"Like some kind of science experiment?"

"Justin, please."

He gave her a cautious sidelong look, then leaned over and planted one on her cheek. She brought a hand up around the back of his neck before he could pull away, and guided his mouth to hers. Their lips met lightly, more of a teasing touch than a kiss, but it made him instantly hard. The pressure of her hand on his neck increased, as did the pressure of her lips when she opened her mouth, inviting him to delve deeper, which he did. Their tongues touched, teased, and then the kiss became almost desperate on her part, as if she was looking for something, seeing if Justin was the guy to give it to her.

Which seemed like a really good plan at the moment.

He pushed his hands into her silky hair, splaying his fingers, holding her head as he kissed her. He hoped she could think straight enough to get the data she needed, because his thought processes were being clouded by the incredible experience of discovering just what Layla felt like, tasted like.

Why had he wasted so much time tormenting her?

Because, as she'd quite correctly deduced, he'd been a totally obnoxious teenage jerk.

Finally, about the time his hands started wandering closer to her breasts, she pulled back, lowering her chin as she met his eyes dead-on, her lower lip slightly swollen, her hair a sexy mess. It was all he could do not to pick her up and carry her off to his room to do this right.

Do what right? He was not sleeping with Layla.

Well, maybe not right off the bat, anyway.

He let out a breath, totally off his game. When had he lost control of the dynamic between them? When had she taken control? *Why* was she taking control?

She frowned slightly, either critically

judging the kiss or getting her bearings. One of the two. Justin didn't need to think in order to pass judgment—pretty much an unexpected ten—but he appreciated the few seconds she gave him to get himself under control.

"Assessment?" he asked softly, hoping to pass this off as an interesting bit of experimentation—which he truly hoped it was.

"Good," she replied.

"Just good?"

She smiled, as if she wasn't buying into his front. It unnerved him to think of his trusty shield no longer working against her.

She ran a hand over her tangled hair, grimaced as she threaded her fingers through it. "A lot of stuff has changed in my life in a short amount of time."

"Is that why you're here?"

"I guess," she said, falling back against the cushions and staring across the room. She brought her forearm up to rest on top of her head. "I lost my job, Justin. I got fired today."

"Fired? I thought you were going to quit."

"I thought I was going to *threaten* to quit." She exhaled heavily, and even though her voice was even, he could see that she was fighting tears. Of course she was. Layla was not the kind of person who would take getting fired in stride. "My principal chose to play hardball. Bad woman to bluff, apparently."

"Damn. Layla. I'm...sorry."

"Me, too. And in case you're wondering, no, I'm not going to take you up on your job offer." She closed her eyes briefly, swallowed hard, and for a moment he thought she was going to let the tears flow. But she didn't. When she turned her head slightly so she could see him, her eyes were shiny, but she was regaining control. "They stole my stuff. Or they're going to."

"What stuff?"

"I spent two years putting together materials and lesson plans for immersion units."

"I don't know what an immersion unit

is, unless we're talking water baths or deep fat fryers."

"An immersion unit is where the kids learn English and history by becoming characters. They act out scenarios. Write about their characters and the events they've witnessed and taken part in. It's very effective."

"Sounds like a hell of a lot of fun." More fun than the history and English classes he remembered. Or rather didn't remember, since he'd spent a lot of time sleeping in them. Or not showing up—until Reggie found out and cleaned his clock.

"I've won awards for the units," she said shortly. "And I developed them on my own time."

"You don't have them on computer?"

"Just some of it. Most of the lessons are only in hard copy."

"I don't get how they can just steal them if you developed the lessons."

"I'll probably get them back—after Melinda copies everything." Layla ground her teeth together. "She can have Robert,

but I do *not* want her using the end result
of two years of my blood, sweat, toil and
tears."

Justin had a simple solution. "Let's go
get them."

FOR A MOMENT Layla simply stared at him.
She'd come here on instinct, kissed him
on instinct. She didn't feel like being arrested on instinct. "I think that would be
construed as breaking and entering or unlawful entry."

"Do you have a key?"

She did. The spare that Derek had made
for her, though she had no idea how, since
the key was not supposed to be duplicated.

"You do have a key," he said, correctly
interpreting her silence.

"What of it?"

"How can it be breaking and entering
if you have a key?"

She made an impatient gesture. "I don't
know."

"Have you ever gone to the school after-
hours? Worked there?"

"About every other day."

"So why not go now. Just like you used to. Get the stuff you really need and beat feet."

"I…"

"Is there an alarm system?"

"Only on the office and the computer lab."

"Security guard?"

"During the day."

"Janitor?"

"Not at night during vacation. They all go on days."

"Sounds like my kind of break-in." He stood, ready for action, the old Justin gleam in his eye. "Let's go. Before the trollop has time to copy them. If you tell me where to find the stuff, I'll go in and get it." He reached down to pick up a small spiral notebook that had a recipe written on the open page. He flipped to a fresh sheet and handed the book to her. "Draw me a map."

She shook her head.

"No? Why not?"

"Because I'm coming with you."

LAYLA HAD ALWAYS suspected that if she embarked on a life of crime, Justin would be involved. And he was. After much debate about what would be less noticeable in the school lot—her car or his—they drove his car to the school and parked next to the Dumpster, out of camera range. Layla knew exactly where the cameras were and what they picked up, thanks to her students. They'd also told her that the security guard didn't always turn them on.

How on earth they knew these things, Layla had no idea, but she hoped they were right and that the cameras weren't on tonight. Even if they were, it was too dark to make out anything.

"Just stay close to this wall and we'll be okay until we hit the doorway. Then we'll be on tape." Her hope was that no one would recognize her in Justin's over-size black sweatshirt, plus a ball cap and sunglasses. She was having a hard time seeing in the sunglasses.

Justin did as he was told, perhaps for the first time in his life, walking along the edge of the building with her, his hand lightly touching the small of her back, making her very, very aware of him.

She kept her head down as she moved onto the back step and fitted her spare key in the lock. It turned smoothly, as always, and she pushed the door open, her heart thumping hard against her ribs. Just a quick in and out, taking only what was hers.

Nothing wrong with that.

The door closed behind them and the motion sensor light in the hall came on, startling both of them. Justin touched her back again and she started moving down the corridor. Her room was at the far end, across from Melinda's, and when Layla opened the door, she could see that someone had already been going through her files. But the person, aka Melinda, hadn't yet found the two storage boxes crammed under the back table beneath the sheets Layla used as togas for the Roman unit.

She bent down and pulled the first box out, and Justin picked it up, putting it on the table. She'd just placed her hand on it when someone walked down the hall, talking on a phone. She instantly froze, her heart hammering, and Justin crouched low beside her, pressing close in the darkness, so close she felt enveloped in his warmth. He nudged her and together they slowly eased under the counter, huddling together, out of sight.

If she got arrested, she was never going to get another teaching job. Breaking and entering a school. What the hell was wrong with her? And Justin couldn't afford to be arrested, either. Not when he worked in a business that relied on reputation.

"What now?" she whispered, her eyes so wide they probably filled her entire face.

The guy paused outside the door and continued to talk. Layla did not recognize the voice, and figured it had to be the new night janitor—the position Ella said she wouldn't be filling until after the students were on vacation. Layla hadn't realized she meant immediately after.

"I cannot believe this is happening."

"It's happening," Justin whispered back. He put an arm over her, drew her even closer. "But he hasn't called the cops."

"How do you know?"

"The call has lasted too long. And he laughed a second ago."

Layla put her head down on her knees and closed her eyes. She felt just like a rabbit, holding very, very still and hoping the hawk didn't see her.

"He's leaving."

Layla raised her head slightly, and sure enough, she could hear the guy walking away, no longer talking. She let out a sigh that seemed to come from the depth of her soul.

"What is it about you and trouble?" she asked.

"*Me* and trouble?" He started out from under the counter, then froze when the door opened and the lights came on. Layla nearly jumped out of her skin as Justin pressed himself back against her, pushing her into the corner, the cold cinder blocks sending a chill through her.

For the first time ever Layla was glad

she had very little storage space in her room and thus a mishmash of cartons and bins under the counters. If she and Justin held very still, then maybe… Her heart was beating so hard it seemed as if the guy should surely be able to hear it.

She could feel Justin's breath on her temple, warm and steady, as if this kind of stuff was old hat for him, which it no doubt was. Layla herself wasn't breathing. She was too afraid.

"Yeah, that's right, baby," the janitor said in a low, purring voice as he pushed his trash can into the room, the wheels squeaking. "I'm going to run my tongue all the way up there."

A nasty feeling rolled over Layla.

The janitor laughed, a low intimate sound, then picked up a wastepaper basket—one that had been empty the last time Layla was in the room—and emptied it, banging it against the side of the larger container. "Yeah, you got a point. Maybe I shouldn't be doing this on my first day of work, but who's gonna catch me?"

Justin nudged Layla, but she ignored him, and the guy laughed again.

"Yeah? You gonna do *that?*"

Layla squeezed her eyes shut, wishing she could close her ears, as well. Please don't say what *that* is....

The bin settled on the floor with a clatter, and then he picked up the second one, next to her former desk, and repeated the action. Melinda, or someone, had been busy in her room.

Maybe the guy was just going to empty the trash and go. He laughed again. "No choice? Oh, I think I have choices. Like where I'm going to start. I know where I'm going to end." He shook out his broom and started making passes around the room as he told the person he was talking to exactly how he was going to get there.

It was the logical place to end, but Layla had never heard it expressed in such graphic terms before. She pressed her face into Justin's arm. Dear heavens.

And Justin, from the way his shoulders shook every now and then, seemed to be laughing.

The broom came within inches of them and Layla drew back as far as she was able, making herself as tiny as possible. Not that the guy would have noticed even if the broom had hit them.

"Oh, stop. You're killing me." He pushed the debris out the door into the hall. "Baby, that is not physically possible...oh, you'll show me?" He started wheeling the squeaky trash can out the door. "I can't, I've just started shift."

Oh, happy day. How long would it take him to clean the rooms in this hallway? Since he'd barely touched this classroom, Layla had hopes of maybe half an hour—unless he got too carried away with his phone conversation.

The lights went out and the door clicked shut.

Layla let out a long, shuddering breath, her body going limp. She'd never in her life been in a situation like this. Had never come close to breaking the law, other than running the occasional yellow light.

It was rather...exhilarating. Especially since they hadn't gotten caught. Maybe she was beginning to understand why people engaged in extreme sports. Or why Justin and her brothers were forever doing stupid stuff with skateboards, bikes, ramps and parachutes.

But she and Justin weren't out of this yet.

"Wow, I didn't know you were allowed to talk like that in a school," he whispered as he settled his back against the wall and stretched his legs out.

"He's newly hired. Perhaps he's not familiar with the rules." Layla assumed a similar position, staring across the darkened room to the bulletin board on the opposite wall. She'd spent a long time on that board, creating a map of the ancient world to tie in with the *Iliad*. She certainly hoped Melinda enjoyed it.

"But he shouldn't be here tonight," Layla moaned. "He should be working days."

"Well, sweetheart, he isn't." Justin put an arm around her, and instead of freezing up, as she would have mere days ago, she leaned her head against his shoulder and accepted his comfort. And when he dropped a light kiss on her hair, she actually smiled.

Maybe she had a knack for crime.

LAYLA WAS NOT FREAKING OUT. Justin had fully expected her to leap out from under the counter and surrender to the dirty-mouthed janitor, and maybe she would have, had the guy been talking about something different.

Justin glanced sideways without moving his head. Gone was the woman he'd thought was in shock before she'd asked him to kiss her. In her place was one Justin didn't believe he'd ever met before. Well, maybe briefly in the parking lot when she'd slugged Robert.

She was scared, which showed a measure of good sense, but she was also calm. Not jittery or fretting or behaving the way he would have predicted she would under these circumstances, had anyone posed a hypothetical question. *Suppose Layla Taylor got caught breaking into a school...*

There was something wrong with this picture.

After a good twenty minutes of staring into space, Justin got out from under the counter and crept across the room. He couldn't see jack out the small slit of a window, so he cautiously eased the door open a crack. Nothing to the south. He took a breath, pushed the door open a bit farther and stuck his head out. Clear to the north.

He motioned with his hand for Layla to join him, and she did, carrying one of the heavy boxes, taking small steps because of the weight.

He grimaced at her. "It's going to be kind of hard to run with one of those."

"I came for my stuff. If I have to I'll drop it." He didn't say anything, but he could see a mutinous expression forming on her face.

"Fine." He crossed over to the counter and hefted the other box, then came back to where she stood, wondering what in the hell she had in these containers. They must weigh about fifty pounds each.

"Okay, let's make a waddle for it."

She laughed. A soft, almost roguish sound. Layla was definitely getting into this.

He opened the door and then quietly closed it after Layla had struggled out with her box. She led the way to the junction of the four hallways, under a domed skylight, and stopped. Justin eased past her and leaned out to check the perpendicular hallways in both directions. The janitor's trash can was parked next to one of the far doors, but Justin couldn't hear anything. He kind of hated to think about what might be happening.

Layla came up beside him and he gestured to the exit with his head. They both started toward the door as fast as their awkward loads would allow. If his arms were straining, hers had to be shaking. And he did not want to have to tell her that if she dropped her box and scattered the contents, they were not going to pick them up. They were getting the hell out of Dodge.

Justin had just opened the outside door when they heard a loud "Hey" from behind them.

"Just getting a few things I forgot to take home," Layla called as she hurried through the door. "Good night!"

They should have parked closer, but Justin hadn't wanted his license plate on camera. Right now he was almost past caring.

They actually were waddling by the time they reached the car. Justin had taken his keys out before he'd grabbed his box so he was able to pop the locks. He braced the box against the rear quarter panel and opened the back door, dumping his load and then taking Layla's and jamming it on top.

She was practically in her seat by the time he'd opened his door. He started the car and backed away, hoping she was right about the cameras.

When he pulled out onto the street, Layla laughed. "Thank you, thank you," she said.

"For the boxes or the adventure?"

"Both." Her eyes were sparkling when he glanced over at her. "I've never, ever experienced anything like that."

"I'm so surprised."

Her eyes were wide when she said, "I'll bet you've done stuff like this before."

"More times than you can imagine." Although this was probably the first time he'd risked arrest as an adult.

Layla laughed again. "I hope Melinda goes crazy trying to find this stuff."

"Do you think she wants it that badly?"

"All the kids wanted to be in my class so they could participate."

"Well, that's an endorsement."

"And in a year or two, she could have pretended she'd developed the material." Layla smiled with an air of satisfaction. "Which is why I'm going to self-publish it. Lots of teachers sell their thematic units. Why not me?"

"Great idea." Justin glanced in his rearview mirror, a habit from his teen days. Only tonight he probably wasn't going to have to pull into a driveway and duck down.

"Let's go get coffee."

"Isn't the adrenaline rush sufficient?" he asked drily.

"I don't want coffee for the caffeine. I just thought perhaps a celebratory drink was in order."

"Coffee schmoffee. Let's go get a real drink."

She didn't answer immediately, and Justin suddenly recalled how they'd hooked up again after all these years. "A beer? No martinis?"

She laughed with a touch of self-consciousness. "A beer sounds good."

He pulled into an off-the-beaten-track pub in a strip mall on Moana Street, and they settled side by side at the bar. Layla was not much of a beer drinker, and it occurred to Justin that she might not be much of a drinker at all. She'd been a teetotaler in high school when the rest of them had been getting blazed at parties.

He noticed her studying their reflection in the mirror behind the bar, and couldn't resist putting his fingers into a V and raising rabbit ears behind her head.

She laughed and slapped at his hand, turning to him to say, "You haven't changed much, have you?"

"No. At this very minute I'm wondering where you keep your bras and where the nearest ROTC flagpole is."

"Definitely one of the stellar memories of my teen years."

"No one knew it was your bra."

"I knew." She put a light hand on his knee, startling him. "Why were you such a jerk to me?"

"Maybe I had a crush on you and that was the only way to express it."

"Really," she said flatly, disbelievingly.

He shrugged. "Or maybe you were a handy target. The studious older sister."

"A bit more believable."

She studied him for a moment, a quizzical look on her face, and with a half smile, Justin reached out to run the tips of his fingers along the smooth skin of her jawline. She shivered and then her eyes widened slightly, as if the reaction had surprised her.

Lovely Layla. Who'd turned out to be a

lot more fun than he'd ever thought possible.

Her beer was still half-full when he finished his, and she pushed it aside as he reached for his wallet. "Done?"

"Done and getting tired. Crime is exhausting."

"Hey—you own that stuff."

"Right." She didn't smile, but he could see the amusement in her eyes.

It was a quiet drive back to his condo and her car, but not an uncomfortable silence. More of a companionable one. Neither spoke as he pulled into his parking spot and then helped transfer the two boxes. When they finished, Layla smiled up at him with a serene, almost sleepy expression.

"It's crazy. I've lost my job and I'm not obsessing."

"I have that effect on women."

She ran her palms up his arms. "I guess you do. The obsessing will come, of course."

"In the early-morning hours, no doubt."

"Is that when *you* obsess?" Layla asked

facetiously, as if making a huge discovery.
"That's when *I* obsess!" He laughed and
she added, "I'll bet I do a lot more of that
than you do."

She might be surprised. He leaned
down and gave her one last kiss, their lips
clinging for a brief second as he made a
wish—that they could explore this unexpected physical connection between them
more fully. "It was great breaking into the
school with you."

"I had a good time, too." She pulled
away and then unlocked her car door.
"Maybe…" She made a face. "I can't believe I'm saying this. Maybe we can do
something together again."

"Maybe. And I can't believe you're
saying that, either."

She reached up and touched the side of
his face lightly, then got into her car and
shut the door. He knocked on the window,
and she rolled it down. "Text me when
you get home."

She nodded and started the engine.

As she pulled away, Justin stood watching, hoping that she understood he was

talking get together in a casual way, not a headed for a relationship way.

But this was Layla, who planned her life to the nth degree. Of course she understood that.

CHAPTER SIX

"Do you know anything about class re-unions?" Sam demanded as soon as Layla walked through the front door of Sunshine of Your Love. She was standing behind the purple checkout counter, small hippie glasses perched on her nose, a sheet of creased paper in one hand.

"I helped plan mine," Layla said. And she'd also broken into a school. Old Layla. New Layla.

Surprisingly, she wasn't riddled with guilt about last night's criminal activity. If anything, she was still slightly exhilarated. For once, she'd stood up for herself, albeit in a clandestine way, and she felt vindicated. Empowered.

Moral of the story? She needed to take control of more areas of her life, instead of playing the good, rule-following girl.

Sam looked over the top of the glasses. "Then word must have spread that the Taylors are suckers for organizing public events, because I've just gotten an invitation to join the planning committee." She pushed her geometrically cut red hair away from one cheek. "I believe I will decline."

"It wasn't that bad," Layla said. "There were several committees, so the workload was spread out."

Sam shook the paper at her. "These guys wanted nothing to do with people like me back in high school, and now they want my help?"

"Perhaps some of them have matured past the clique days?"

"Oh, I don't know. Carlie McCoy was in here the other day and she was pretty damned condescending."

"Did she buy anything?"

"Loads of fancy underwear and a pair of novelty guy underwear on clearance. The Christmas kind."

"Rudolph?"

"The elf hat."

Sam shoved the paper into the folder next to the register, where she kept her special order list. "I just can't see hanging with those people." There was the briefest of pauses and then she casually said, "Have you heard from Mom?"

"Not recently." Their parents were currently living in Hawaii, house-sitting for a friend for several months and enjoying life in paradise. "Is everything all right?" Layla asked, suspecting from her sister's change in demeanor that something was up.

Sam didn't quite meet her eyes. Never a good sign. "Well, I may have let the cat out of the bag about your job, so you'll probably be getting a call from her."

Layla instantly felt shifty. Not for keeping her mother in the dark, but because she, queen of the overachievers, had lost her job. Walked away from her contract. And now she had to explain this to people. Was she going to tell her mother that Robert had been sleeping with someone else? No. She and her mom simply didn't discuss things like that. Not that her mother hadn't tried…. Layla was simply too private.

But Sam wasn't. Their mom probably already knew.

"What did she say?" Layla asked, curious as to whether she'd be happy Layla was breaking free, and if so, why she hadn't gotten a congratulatory call. The time difference, perhaps?

"I think she's worried. You're the anal, responsible child and shouldn't be getting fired. That's what the rest of us do. You're the one kid Mom didn't have to worry about."

What? "But she always seemed so frustrated that I didn't celebrate freedom like the rest of you." Layla distinctly remembered her mother urging her to ease up on herself, have a little fun.

"She probably thought you were going to explode from self-imposed rules." Sam pulled the duster out from under the counter and started attacking the jewelry display. "And now she thinks the explosion has occurred."

"It has."

Sam looked up, duster poised in the air. "For real?"

"It feels like it." Layla walked over to an oak table Sam had "borrowed" from their parents' house while they were in Hawaii. It was now covered in bustiers, bras and panties. "Or rather, it feels like I've suddenly realized that there's more than one path a person can follow, and I want to explore a little before settling onto a single pathway again."

"What exactly are you saying?" Sam asked, her eyes wide. "Could it be that you're actually following my advice?"

"Kind of." Layla tidied a stack of panties. "I'm going to summer school in June and maybe back to college full-time next fall." It had taken her a couple days and one sleepless night to come to that firm decision. Educational credits had soared in price since she'd last attended school, but she had a tidy sum in Grandma Bonnie's legacy bank account, and Layla was certain she was the only one of the four Taylor grandchildren who hadn't spent the lot. She'd saved it for a rainy day, and the rain was now officially falling.

"Master's degree in education?" Sam asked drily.

So much for being unpredictable. Layla picked up a pale pink bustier from a display table and held it against her. "I don't know."

"You don't know?" Sam settled the hand with the duster on her cocked hip, an expression of patent disbelief on her face. "And by the way, that color suits you."

Layla dropped the bustier back onto the table. "All right," she said irritably. "Yes, I'm thinking of a master's in ed. If I can get into grad school." Which shouldn't be a problem, since she'd graduated university cum laude. "I sent my application in this morning."

"This is not a different path," Sam pointed out.

"I like kids. I think I should stay in teaching." If she hadn't screwed up her career too much by getting herself fired. She picked up the sliver of satin that matched the bustier and dangled it from one finger, trying to figure out what went where. A thong? Maybe. Not much to it.

"Just remember there are other careers than the one you chose when you were five—even if you do like kids." Sam dabbed the duster at the branches of a brass tree that held crystal bracelets. "After all, I like flowers, but that doesn't mean I should spend my life arranging them."

"I will try to keep an open mind."

No. She *would* keep an open mind. But she also needed to make a living eventually, and continuing in education was her best bet. Perhaps she'd be adventurous in other areas of her life. Like, say, the man area? In the form of one Justin Tremont?

As crazy as it was, Layla was beginning to think Justin was the best thing that had happened to her in a while. Because of his help retrieving what was rightfully hers, aka breaking into the school and taking her lessons, she felt a sense of power she hadn't experienced in, well, forever.

"Could you give me a hand while we debate about your future?" Sam asked, putting the duster away. She was still struggling to get back on her feet after the bead shop debacle, and couldn't afford to hire help, so Layla did what she could, as did her brothers. Sam had borrowed money from them to get this new shop started, and was bound and determined not to screw up again.

"I can give you a few hours, and we don't need to discuss my future. I'm going to summer school unless the perfect job appears, which, given the current economic climate, is highly unlikely."

"I agree," Sam said.

"What do you want me to do?"

"I have some dresses in the back that need steaming and a couple boxes of lingerie to put on hangers."

Layla set her purse behind the counter and headed to the back room to turn on the steamer.

"I wonder if Derek or Eric got a reunion planning invite?" Sam said musingly, unfolding the letter once again. Since she'd been born a mere ten months after the twins, they were all in the same graduation class. Sam and the boys were practically triplets. Layla had always been the odd child out. By age. By temperament.

Nothing she could change about the age, but the temperament…yes, she'd be doing some work in that area.

"I can ask Justin if he got one next time I see him." He'd graduated the same year as Sam—one year after Layla—and he and Sam had run with the same rowdy crowd.

"Why on earth would you be seeing Justin?" Sam called from the other room.

"We went out a couple nights ago."

"Like on a date?"

Layla was not telling Sam about the school. She wasn't going to tell anyone she'd done something of questionable legality. "I stopped by his place to tell him I'd gotten fired, and he took me out for a beer."

"Justin," Sam said, as Layla came out from behind the beaded curtains. "Tremont. The guy you wanted to fire from a cannon when we were younger?"

Layla felt unexpectedly self-conscious. "That's the one."

"That doesn't seem right."

"May I point out that you're the person responsible for us getting together again after all these years?"

"That was because of an emergency." Sam pushed her hair away from her cheek with a distracted gesture.

"Regardless of why, somehow…well… things have changed."

"How?" Sam demanded.

She wasn't ready to share all the details. Not just yet. "Maybe we're just looking at each other differently."

"Like…*differently* differently?" her sister asked with a significant lift of her eyebrows.

"In a way."

But instead of laughing, as Sam always did when confronted with an unexpected twist in life, she went quiet. So quiet that Layla said, "What?"

She gave a quick shake of her head. "Nothing. Just, well, you know that Justin is never serious about anything."

Layla simply stared at her sister for a moment. Sam was trying to keep her from being hurt. As if Justin could possibly hurt her.

She gave a soft snort. "Trust me, Sam. I'm not looking for anything serious. I've done serious for way too long. It sucks."

All she wanted to do was to shake off her tight-assed tendencies, and Justin seemed like the man to help her.

"WHAT'S WRONG WITH YOU lately?" Eden asked, coming into the pastry room, where Justin was arranging the dowels he'd be using to support the layers of a three-tier cake he'd be delivering the next day.

He gave her a mystified look. He'd been quiet and focused on his work, but, as far as he knew, not overtly troubled. "Nothing."

Eden shook her head. "Okay, you're working way too many hours." She shifted her weight and folded her arms over her chest. "Which is normal, I guess.

But you're too quiet and you haven't been playing music."

"What do you want to hear?" he asked.

Eden let out a weary sigh. "I don't want to hear anything, but I want to know why all the deep thinking? The last time you were like this was when Dad and Reggie had that big fight and he disappeared. Forever."

Justin silently groaned. How did he explain that he'd been doing his deep thinking about a child his sister didn't even know existed? That last night he'd looked at photos of himself at the same age of ten and wondered what his son looked like? That he was starting to obsess over something he couldn't control and it was driving him nuts. Justin was one step away from searching crowds for faces similar to his own.

He set down the cake armature and went to put his hands on his sister's shoulders. "You know what? I can honestly handle my own life. I have some things to think about. Condo balloon payments, for one."

"Cindy for another?"

He shook his head. Eden's shoulders slumped. "I know it's none of my business, but when you go silent, it bothers me."

"I'll be noisier," he said, forcing a smile that wouldn't fool his sister. "And if I have a serious problem, you'll be the first to know. This is just a bunch of small stuff."

Big lie.

"This is all about condo payments?"

"And exhaustion."

"I don't believe you," she said in a sing-song voice.

"That doesn't matter," he said, mimicking her tone. Should he tell her it *was* about Cindy? Because that was what she wanted to hear. Couldn't do it. One big lie between them was enough. "I'm fine. Honest. I just need to get a little more sleep."

"When will that happen?" Eden asked darkly.

"Just as soon as I can quit at the lake. After the balloon payment." Which he'd been saving for diligently and would make right on schedule—when his kid was twelve years old.

And in the meanwhile, Justin needed to loosen up. Act normally. Or Eden was going to drive him insane…unless he could somehow distract her.

LAYLA SPENT SEVERAL HOURS Thursday morning helping Sam unpack a giant order, then watched the store while her sister went on a chai tea latte run. One last Fed Ex delivery came while Sam was gone, and Layla sliced open the first box, then started checking the contents against the invoices. Body jewelry. Amusing cards. Colored condoms.

Oh, this is interesting.

She pulled out a smaller container with a picture of the device inside, something that looked very much like a space-age cat toy. Only it wasn't. The Rocket Launcher. Apparently it must be a bestseller, since Sam had ordered ten of them.

Layla started lining the boxes up on the table in front of her and found she was one short.

She was digging deeper in the container, pulling out the packing material, when the bells on the front door jangled. Sam with the tea. And not a moment too soon, because Layla was running on empty caffeine-wise.

"We're missing a Rocket Launcher," she called as the footsteps stopped on the other side of the counter.

"How many do you need?" a masculine voice inquired.

Layla gave a small shriek and looked up to meet Justin's laughing eyes.

"You scared me!" she said, pressing her hand to her chest to try and slow her racing heart.

"I'm sorry. There was no one out front."

"I know, but most customers don't wander into the back room." Layla's heart was still racing, and it was because of those damned Rocket Launchers. She and Justin and sex toys…

He picked up the box and read the back. "Guaranteed, huh?"

Layla cleared her throat. "Sam likes top-of-the-line gizmos."

"Gizmos?" he asked, lifting one brow. "Devices?"

He smiled, and she cocked her head with a slight frown, feeling the need to change the subject. "What are you doing here?"

"I had a cake delivery down the street at the lodge hall, saw your car and thought I'd stop by and see if there were any repercussions from our visit to the school."

"None," she said as she started putting the Rocket Launchers back in the larger container, practically yanking the last one out of Justin's grasp. "But I did spend the past two days expecting a cop to show up at my door."

Justin laughed. "Would you believe I'm very familiar with that feeling? Welcome to the dark side." He leaned his forearms on the counter, clasped his really nice hands together. "Committed any other crimes lately?"

"I drove too fast coming over here," she said with a tiny smile. The bells jingled again and Sam came in, carrying the tea.

"Oh, Justin. Hi." She looked from Layla

to him and back again, a huge question in her eyes, then put on her customer smile. "Are you shopping?"

"Stopped by to see Layla, but I should be going."

"Actually, me, too," Layla said, taking one of the cups of tea. She had chores to catch up on at home and was still working on her résumé, just in case a job appeared on the horizon. She might be searching for a new path, but she was also going to be prepared for every eventuality.

"And by the way," she said in an aside, "you're missing a Rocket Launcher. Only nine in the shipment."

"I'll call the company," Sam replied, coming around the counter to take Layla's place. She did not seem happy.

"What?" Layla mouthed silently, as Justin pushed the curtains aside.

Sam made a dismissive gesture with one hand. "See you tomorrow?" she asked.

"Nine o'clock," Layla responded. *Be prepared to give answers.*

Layla and Justin headed out of the back

room and toward the exit, telling herself that if she had the guts to arrive at his door unannounced and kiss him, then there was no reason she couldn't just ask him out again. This time without unlawful entry being involved.

Just ask.

Except that it was harder than she thought. Too many years of conditioning. They were almost to the door when his phone rang. He pulled it out of his pocket and groaned when he saw the number.

"This can't be good," he muttered before he said hello. Then he tipped his head back and closed his eyes as if in pain. "Are you freaking kidding me?"

Layla could clearly hear a "no," then a bunch of garbled words.

"All right, I'll come back. Yes. Right now. Yes." He shut the phone off and muttered. "I'm also charging you."

"What happened?"

Justin held the door open and Layla walked out into the sunny parking lot. "They dropped something on the cake.

Smashed the flowers on one side. Now I have to go do damage control."

Layla walked with him as far as the Tremont van, doing some quick calculations in her head as to times and places, and then said, "Can I come and watch?"

He turned to her with one hand on the door handle and gave her an odd look.

Was she coming off as a pastry groupie or something? "I've never seen a cake rescue before," she said coolly.

"And you want to watch the master at work?"

"Actually," Layla said seriously, adjusting her purse strap on her shoulder, "that has always been a dream of mine."

Justin smiled briefly. "Then you're in luck, because I like to have an audience whenever possible." He opened the van door and jerked his head toward the interior. "Come on. Let's go rescue a cake."

Less than five minutes later they parked behind a lodge hall four blocks away, then went into the kitchen through the back door, Justin carrying the box of supplies he'd used an hour before to set up the cake.

"Oh, thank goodness you're here." A plump woman in a pink dress rushed up to them, gesturing dramatically across the room. There, sitting on the counter near the refrigerator, was a multilayer cake, the flowers on one side smashed into a mess of red and pink.

"Can you save it?" Layla whispered. She was amazed that Justin had created the cake in the first place. It was three tiers high, with flowers cascading down the side and spun sugar butterflies nestled between the blossoms.

Justin's mouth tightened as he surveyed the damage. "It's not going to be one hundred percent."

The woman's hand fluttered up to her chest. "Will it be close?"

"It won't be ugly," he said.

With a great deal of tact and reassurance, he managed to get the woman to leave the kitchen, along with the other three people who'd popped in to see if he could work a miracle.

"You're honestly going to fix this," Layla said doubtfully.

"Have some faith, woman." Then he set to work, removing the damaged flowers, resurfacing the cake with cream-colored icing, filling in the dips and dents. When he was done, he mixed red and pink frosting on a plate, loaded his piping bag with a scoop of each and started making roses with masterful precision.

Layla leaned on the counter, completely absorbed. She'd once watched him replace bearings in skateboard wheels, and he used to tinker with Eric's old Chevy for hours, fixing things that neither twin could. But frosting? How on earth had he gotten into this line of work? And become so good at it?

"Do you ever get crap about making cakes and frosting flowers?"

"Of course," Justin said, putting the final petals on a rose, then immediately starting another.

"Does it bother you?"

He gave a small, dismissive snort. "I'm comfortable with who I am. I like making cakes, and if you haven't noticed, I'm pretty good at it. I don't care what people think."

Layla studied her clasped hands for a moment. "I guess I should try to become more like you in that regard."

Justin's focus remained on the cake as he said, "Perhaps so."

Layla's mouth flattened slightly. "If you had told me even a year ago that I would be using you as my role model, I would have laughed."

"No…you would have laughed, but deep down you might have suspected that I wasn't that bad of a role model." He finished the rose and stood back to view the effect.

"Why do you say that?"

He stopped piping. "Because when we had a chance to get the hell out of that school the other night, you insisted on carrying hundred-pound boxes and risking capture."

"They didn't weigh a hundred pounds."

Carrying his piping bag, he walked over to where she stood next to his equipment box. "I think you are more like me than you want to admit. There are parts of you that have been tamped down for so long they seem foreign to you." When she didn't answer, Justin picked up another bag, loaded it with green icing and began making leaves.

"Can you teach me to do that?"

"Only if you're more talented than Eden. She's the worst."

Layla laughed and Justin smiled over at her, their gazes connecting in an intimate way that startled her. It was quite apparent to her that he had noticed.

"This is still a little strange to me," she said, feeling the need to confess. "I never expected us to ever be…I don't know. *Friends* doesn't seem like the right word."

"No," he agreed matter-of-factly. "It doesn't." The way he looked at her made something stir inside her.

She tucked a few strands of hair behind her ear, suddenly wondering if she should have kept her mouth shut. "So what do you call the guy who keeps me from thinking about my cheating ex-boyfriend and getting fired and—" She broke off abruptly when he lifted the pastry bag and put a tiny dot of frosting on her lower lip.

"Gets you thinking about…other stuff?"

Somehow she found her breath. "Maybe a little."

He leaned in to lick off the dot with the tip of his tongue, and her body went liquid. "I don't know what you call that guy."

His smile faded away as he touched her frosting-free top lip with his tongue. A tingling chill shot through her as her eyes drifted closed. She kept them shut, waiting for whatever came next.

She felt his breath on her mouth before she felt his lips. "I thought you didn't mix business and—"

His mouth closed over hers in a hard kiss that drew a response from her toes on up. Dear heavens. He backed her against the counter as he deepened the kiss.

When he finally raised his head, Layla's

chest rose and fell heavily as she drew in a deep breath and exhaled. Heaving bosom. Compliments of Justin Tremont.

"Oh, you're done!" The pink lady bustled into the room, followed by two other ladies, one dressed in green, one in blue. They looked a bit like the three fairies in the *Sleeping Beauty* movie.

"Not quite," Justin said, his eyes on Layla.

She focused on the women, wondering how much they'd seen, and telling herself it really didn't matter. So she was making out with their pastry chef. Big deal.

But parts of her body were saying it was a very big deal. Justin was one hot chef.

As LAYLA STEPPED AWAY from him, Justin knew he had to be careful—and not because he'd just shocked the hell out of his clients, who were pretending they hadn't just witnessed the end of a major lip-lock as they *oohed* and *ahhed* over the cake.

Frankly, he was glad they'd come in when they did.

The plan had been to treat Layla like

any other woman he was attracted to. Ask her out a few times, give himself something to think about, and more than that, to give Eden something else to think about. And so far, so good. No—so far, *too* good.

He shifted slightly in an effort to adjust himself.

The ladies stayed in the kitchen, either to guard the cake or to make certain there was no more hanky-panky, as Justin rinsed and then packed his tools. Layla stood to the side, waiting for him to finish, but she was close enough that he could still smell her perfume. It made him want to lean closer to her. Close his eyes. Bury his nose in the hollow of her neck and simply inhale.

That worried him.

But why? After all, she'd made it clear that she was only looking for fun, that serious wasn't in the game plan. Exactly his kind of woman. Except that kissing Layla felt different than kissing other women. Also, because he knew for a fact that he'd eventually walk away, it also felt a hell of a lot as though he was using her to stop himself from fixating on his child.

He didn't like that feeling one bit.

LAYLA HAD NO IDEA what to expect when they left the lodge hall fifteen minutes later, but it wasn't Justin saying, "I'll drop you at your car. I have to get back to the kitchen."

"Sure." She sounded wonderfully unconcerned, but her body was still dealing with the aftermath of the frosting kiss. The heat of his mouth on hers... the promise of how much more he had to offer. Talk about an excellent distraction. Why waste time worrying about the future when she had the promise of hot sex?

And a little hot sex would take the sting out of Robert's assessment of her tight-assed abilities.

"Would you like to go out again?" Layla asked in an amazingly nonchalant voice as he pulled the van to a stop next to her car.

"Why? You planning to knock over a bank or something?"

She gave him a look. "No. I thought it would be fun to go out."

He shrugged, then smiled, but he seemed hesitant, and Layla almost said, "Never mind." But she didn't. She kept her mouth firmly shut, waited for a reply and finally got one.

"I'm busy this weekend filling in at the lake for a chef…."

"Tomorrow?" she said. "Maybe we could meet at Nia's Lounge? Around seven?"

"You want to meet?"

She nodded. "Yes. I think that will work best."

There was another healthy pause, and then he said, "Sure."

Sure. Just…sure. And not even a smile to go with it, but Layla wasn't going to let that slow her down. She was a woman on a mission and if the catering van hadn't been so wide, with a huge console between the seats, she would have leaned over and kissed his cheek. Or lips. Whatever was handy.

Instead, she said, "See you then," and

got out. Justin drove away a few seconds later and Layla walked back to her car without going into the store to see Sam.

He hadn't seemed wild about going out with her. Why he was hesitating after that hot kiss, she had no idea, and if he'd been any other guy, she probably would have backed off.

But Justin made her curious.

CHAPTER SEVEN

JUST A SIMPLE DATE. Nothing more. Layla was no different than any other woman he'd dated. They'd have some fun, go their separate ways. She knew that. He knew that.

So why did he feel so unsettled at the prospect of going out with her for real? As in a planned date? Even if it would distract Eden.

He wasn't going to experiment on Layla.

Justin drove to the kitchen and carted his cake supplies inside, thinking life was easier when he became involved with women he liked and found sexy, but didn't have any kind of strong feelings for— even if those feelings were only protective brotherly ones.

Brotherly. Ha. Nice try.

Okay. Not brotherly. But protective.

And who was he protecting her from? Himself. Because he would only let himself get so close to people before he backed off, and doing that with Layla might be messier than it had been in his other relationships. They had a history.

But on the other hand, Layla was a grown woman who could take care of herself. He'd be up-front about his limitations going in. Honesty was the best policy....

Ha! Who was he to talk about honesty?

Not a simple situation.

Reggie was in the office and Eden at the stove. Patty, his trusted aide-de-camp, was in the pastry room, frosting a cake that he should have started working on a half hour ago—and would have, had it not been for the emergency at the lodge hall.

"What took you so long?" Eden asked over her shoulder.

"They dropped something on the cake. I had to go back and fix it."

She grimaced and turned back to the stove. Patty, on the other hand, put down her spatula and pulled a note card from the pocket of her starched apron.

Justin set his box of supplies on the counter and waited for the rundown. Patty was in her mid-forties, no-nonsense, strict in her habits and totally devoted to him getting his cakes out on time. And she was very afraid that when she went to have surgery, he and his sisters would hire a temp they found more efficient than her.

"This morning I got a call from the planner for the Lawrence wedding, who wants a call back regarding the color of the flowers on the cake topper…."

Justin listened and nodded at the appropriate times, until Patty handed him the note card, which he placed in his own pocket.

"Thanks, Patty. I don't know what I'd do without you."

She gave a satisfied nod, picked up her spatula and went back to work, leaving Justin to wash his utensils and continue his Layla debate.

Layla had, without a doubt, the most boring closet this side of a boarding school. Slacks, blouses, skirts. A few

T-shirts for working around the house. The black silk cocktail dress she'd worn on that life-altering night up at Lake Tahoe.

She was getting sick and tired of looking like an escapee from an L.L. Bean catalog. Not that there was anything wrong with Bean, but she wanted to look a bit more Victoria's Secret. In a sedate kind of way. And without spending a lot of money. Or any money.

She punched number two on her phone. Sam answered almost immediately. "What's up?" she asked on a yawn.

"I need a dress for a date. Do you have anything that'll work for me?"

"Are you going out with Justin?"

"I'm looking for some fun." And a bit of seduction. Perhaps even something more, in the future.

Right now she was happy with rebound, but as she'd reflected over the kitchen incident, she'd realized there were things about Justin that she found very attractive now that he'd matured. Things other than his nicely muscled body and handsome face.

"Fun is a reasonable goal," Sam allowed.

"And you've got to admit that Justin knows how to have fun." Plus, he was pretty good with a piping bag. "So do you have anything that's not pornographic?"

"Ye-e-s," Sam said in a "duh" tone of voice. Layla could just picture the withering expression on her sister's face. "Tell you what. Bring me something to eat and we can go through my closet."

"Just part of it. I don't have time for the whole thing."

"I'll pull out some possibilities before you get here."

"Thanks, Sam."

Before she hung up, Sam said, "You know, if you're looking for fun, my friend Willie—"

"I don't think so," Layla said rapidly. Willie was an attractive man, but had the unfortunate habit of humming or singing whenever the urge hit him.

"See you in a few." Layla hung up and went for her jacket, hoping her sister had something that didn't look like she was about to turn a trick or attend a midnight Druid ritual.

Forty-five minutes later, Sam was fed and Layla was contemplating the two-foot-high pile of dresses on her bed.

"Wow. Do you wear all these?"

"At least once." Sam shrugged. "A girl has to have a hobby," she said as she lifted the dress on top. "I'm still working on you and Justin dating."

"Not dating. Just going out."

Sam held the green dress with the silver gauze overlay against her chest, spreading the skirt with one hand.

"Possible," Layla said.

Sam laid the dress over a chair and then lifted what looked like a spangled red tube, about four inches wide.

"No."

"You need to see it on. I have this velvet cape that goes over it."

"No capes."

Sam shrugged and put it back in the small space she'd cleared in her jammed closet—one of two. The next dress was black and shimmery. Layla didn't feel like shimmering. The one after that was iridescent blue, with a neckline that went almost to the hem.

"This one wasn't supposed to be in here," Sam said. "Not a Justin dress."

"Are you sure it really *is* a dress?" And what did her sister mean, not a Justin dress? It looked perfect for what Layla had in mind.

"You wear a lace tube under it," Sam explained. "But guys really like it when you don't."

"Oh, I can imagine." After a brief moment, she said, "Why are you so weird about me and Justin?"

"Because it is weird?" She held up a pink, fluttery dress that reminded Layla of the eighties.

"Pass."

"You're a hard sell, girl."

"I need something tasteful, but daring in a sedate way."

"You mean boringly daring?"

Layla laughed and stretched her arms over her head, taking the kinks out of her back. Funny how she didn't have those stress backaches anymore. "I guess."

"I happen to have, in this stack, my latest boringly daring number." Sam pulled a dark green dress from near the bottom of the pile, stretching the fabric until it came free, and held it up.

"No."

"Try it on."

"It's—"

"Try. It. On." Sam shoved the hanger at her. Layla took it, laid it over the zebra chair next to her and peeled out of her khakis and blouse.

"Dear heavens," Sam said. "Where do you buy your underwear?"

Layla rolled her eyes. "Not at your place, obviously."

"Well, I'll be sending some samples over for you to try."

Layla looked down at her totally fine underwear. It wasn't as if she was wearing granny panties. Beige cotton bikini and bra. She happened to like cotton. She looked back up at her sister. "I cannot be the only woman on this planet who hates the feel of a thong up her…well, you know."

"Whatever." Sam handed her the dress and Layla looked it over for a moment before Sam said, "Just put it on over your head."

Layla lifted her arms and did so, smoothing the elasticized ruching as she tugged the heavy jersey fabric downward. The dress clung, but didn't squeeze. She glanced up at the mirror, surprised that she didn't look like a sausage, as she'd anticipated. The bodice dipped low in a V and the body clung to her torso and hips, where the skirt fell away in deep folds.

Yes. This would do.

Sam was smiling her superior smile as she leaned against the bedpost. "Told you," she said.

"Have you worn this?" Layla asked.

"Haven't had the chance, and now I'll never get to because I'm giving it to you."

Layla half turned, enjoying the feel of the jersey as it swirled around her legs. "Thank you, Sam. I accept."

"Great. Then maybe you can help me

get these class reunion people off my back. I've finally figured out what's going on. There aren't that many of us left in town and I'm one of the lucky few."

"Justin's still in town."

"Maybe I'll sic them on him. They said they're looking for someone artistic to help with the dinner dance decorations."

"Well, you are artsy, Sam."

"I don't know," she said. "David Heinz wouldn't even look at me in high school, refused to acknowledge me as a person, and now he needs my artistic skills."

"People change," Layla said. She had firsthand evidence of that. She'd changed. Justin had changed. "And you can always keep saying no."

"Easier said than done. This guy is persistent."

"And so are you. I have the utmost faith in your ability to persevere."

"At least one of us does," Sam said wearily. She picked up a dress and put it on a hanger. "Want to help me restore order?"

"You bet." It was the least she could

do after scoring a gorgeous dress and refusing to help her sister with the reunion storm troopers.

THE SITUATION WITH LAYLA was driving Justin nuts. On the one hand, being a guy, he wanted to sleep with her, wanted to explore the unexpected chemistry between them. On the other hand, after hours of trying to convince himself otherwise, he knew that he couldn't just have sex with her a few times, then walk away. Not with Layla.

She'd want a reason as to why they were ending things—unless she had the brains to call it off first. He'd lie to her, because he had to.

Things would go from bad to worse. Her brothers would beat the crap out of him…or at the very least think a hell of a lot less of him.

It would be better, much better, to simply end things now, when all they'd shared were a few hot kisses and an unlawful entry. Possibly theft. He wasn't certain where the law stood on Layla removing her own belongings from a place she was banned from.

But eventually it all came down to the lie.

He and Rachel and her parents were the only ones who knew the truth. If he formed a relationship with Layla and allowed it to become serious, as his gut told him it would, the lie would always be there between them. Even if she never knew, he would.

How did a person build trust in a relationship when he wasn't worthy of trust?

LAYLA WALKED THE SIX blocks to Nia's Lounge, glad that she'd suggested meeting him there, rather than having him pick her up. It was in keeping with the type of date she wanted this to be—casual, nonthreatening. If she was reading him right, Justin was a bit concerned about her intentions—and well he should be, because they were not entirely pure. But she wasn't going to push things. Much. Yet.

A server greeted her when she walked in. "I think your table is free." Layla had a favorite table and came often enough that the people working there knew which it was—the one under the corner windows.

"Thanks, but I'm waiting for someone."

She didn't have to wait long. Justin came in the door a few seconds later, looking pretty damned good in jeans and a white shirt, with a brown corduroy blazer.

"Wow," he said, standing back to take a look at her.

She smiled. "Likewise." He put his hand at her elbow and they went into the bar, then Layla stopped. Stared.

No.

Nia's had always been her place. She'd started going there in college, when a friend's family had owned it, and had continued to go after they'd sold. She'd introduced Robert to Nia's, and while he'd seemed to like it, she hadn't thought he'd be there. With Melinda, who was leaning across the small table to hear whatever it was he was saying.

Justin followed her gaze, then said, "Let's go."

"No." Layla gave an adamant shake of her head. "I'm not going to dodge Robert. Especially since we live in the same neighborhood."

"I don't think this is a good idea."

Layla ignored him and walked across the lounge. She stopped close to the table, enjoying both Robert's and Melinda's shocked looks. Justin joined her, although she could practically hear his weary internal sigh.

"How's business, Robert?"

"Good." His handsome face took on its professional mask. Melinda looked positively smug. Not one inkling of discomfort. She had, after all, taken the victory on many fronts.

"Did you get that contract you'd hoped for?" Layla asked.

"Uh, yes," he said, his lips barely moving. "That worked out nicely."

She idly fingered the long pearl necklace she wore. "Many things have worked out nicely for you lately."

"You, too, I see," Melinda said, nodding

at Justin as if Layla getting another guy so soon made what she'd done all right.

The crazy thing was that on some level it did.

"So," Robert said to Justin, "I understand you're a baker or cook or something?"

He made it sound as if Justin had one of the many fine fast-food jobs available in the city.

"How'd you know that?"

"Research after our encounter at Lake Tahoe."

"Ah," Justin said, as if a major mystery had been solved. "Yeah. I am."

"Pretty interesting occupation, making flowers out of frosting and such." Condescension radiated from Robert's arrogant expression.

"It pays the bills."

"Does it really?" Melinda asked with apparent interest. She was good. Layla couldn't decide if she was actually interested or being condescending, as well.

"A large custom cake will run in the thousands," Justin said.

"Really? I had no idea." Melinda cocked her head thoughtfully.

Robert said nothing, but Layla could see that he hadn't realized cakes cost so much.

"How many do you do?"

"Enough that I don't get much sleep," Justin said.

"I like your dress," Melinda said. "I think I saw it in the window of your sister's porn shop."

Layla went still at the unprovoked assault, her breath catching. Had the trollop just said that to her? But she recovered almost immediately, raising her eyebrows politely. "I didn't know you were a customer. I'll have to see that Sam sends you some promotional coupons."

"I wouldn't set foot in there," Melinda said mildly, putting her nose in the air. "I don't need implements."

"It isn't a matter of needing, but rather of enhancing. And with some men..." Layla paused significantly, shooting the smallest of glances at Robert "...you might appreciate a little enhancement."

Layla couldn't believe she'd just said

that, and apparently, judging from the look on his face, neither could Robert. She was turning into Sam. Or maybe the dress imparted special powers.

"Layla, this has been loads of fun," Justin said, taking her by the arm, "but we need to go."

"But—"

"Good night," he said to Robert and Melinda, before steering Layla firmly toward the door.

When they hit the street, she said, "Maybe that wasn't such a good idea."

"No. I think you got some closure, which was what you were after. Right?"

"Right."

He put an arm around her as they walked down the street toward his car. "Wanna go get rip-roaring drunk?"

She laughed and leaned into him. "No. That just gets me into trouble." Had she ever felt this connected with Robert? Never. But Justin was right—she had needed the closure. "But I wouldn't mind a drink."

Heaven knew she wanted one.

JUSTIN WOULD HAVE dearly loved to pop Robert what's-his-name in the face for bringing Melinda to a bar that Layla obviously thought of as her place. Not only that, he was taken aback by the rather primal protective instincts that had ripped through him when the bitch made that remark about Sam's "porn shop," even though Layla had handled the situation masterfully.

Extreme protectiveness.

Probably not a good sign.

Ceol was Justin's favorite bar, even though he hadn't had as much time to hang out there as he used to. They made their way inside, past the dartboard, where two young guys were deep into a game, an Akita dog sitting next to one.

"There's a dog in here," Layla whispered.

"His name is Seby. He's a regular."

Her eyebrows shot up. "How often do you come to this place?"

Justin smiled down at her. "Quite often up until about a year ago. Since the cakes took off, I haven't had time to do much of anything except work, eat and sleep."

"How about your social life?"

"I squeeze that in here and there."

"Justin!" A guy appeared out of the crowd to clap his arm. Layla gave him a how-much-time-do-you-really-spend-here look.

"Good to see you," Justin said, before introducing Layla.

"What'll you have?" he asked. "I can't get you a seat just yet, but I can get you a drink."

"Beer okay?" Justin asked.

"Fine."

"Two Smithwick's."

"You got it." They stood next to the wall, watching the dart game. "I don't think they're following the rules," Layla said.

"Sometimes it's more fun not to follow the rules. Flaunt authority."

"You've never been much for authority," Layla agreed.

"And you have."

"Authority comforts me. Follow the rules and all will be well."

"How's that worked out?"

"Really good up until recently, but it wasn't like I didn't pay a price for sticking to the straight and narrow."

"Yeah?"

"I'm not even certain how high a price. I've been afraid of losing control of my life for so long.... I don't even know where the fear came from. My brothers and sisters? Fearless."

"Derek maybe. Eric? He wienered out on a few things."

"Roof? Skateboard?"

"Among other fine adventures." Many of which had involved getting a rise out of Layla. It couldn't have been easy being the responsible older child when her three younger siblings were such hellions and, because Sam was barely ten months younger than the twins, all in the same grade. Her siblings were like the three musketeers. Throw himself into the mix and... Justin let out a breath. "Would you believe I'm sorry for the crap we—I—did to you?"

"No." She leaned against him, their shoulders and upper arms touching. And stayed like that as she studied the bar patrons.

Justin finally gave in to temptation and put his arm around her shoulders, drawing her close, telling himself to stop now. But she was soft and warm and smelled fantastic.... No biggie. Two people snuggled together, waiting for a table, watching the crowd while becoming superaware of one another. Of the moment. Of possibilities.

He realized then that it wasn't the here and now that was concerning him. It was the future. With Layla he felt as if he could skip a couple steps. Fast-forward because he knew her so well.

Fast-forward to where?

Therein lay the rub.

Every one of Justin's relationships followed the same path. If he fast-forwarded, the only place he had to go was to the end.

Layla smiled up at him, looking, well, beautiful in a way he'd never appreciated when he was younger. His arm tightened for a second before the owner of the bar came up to them and said, "There's a free table near the rear entrance."

"Thanks, Ron."

"Do you know everyone here?" Layla asked as his arm fell away.

"Pretty much." Justin held out a chair for her and had barely sat down himself when someone hailed him. He turned in his chair to see Paula Diaz, former cheerleader and senior class secretary, waving at him. He waved back without much enthusiasm, then noticed she was sitting with at least six other people from their graduating class.

Damn.

The reunion committee. He'd received a letter a while back asking for help, but had no intention of even going to a reunion. He had no good memories of his last year of high school. Not one.

"You okay?" Layla asked when he turned back.

"Yeah. Just some people from high school."

Layla narrowed her eyes as she looked over his shoulder at the group. "I recognize a couple of them. Would that be the infamous reunion committee?"

"How do you know that?"

"David Heinz is there. He's after Sam, trying to take advantage of her artistic abilities. And I remember Paula. Kind of."

"Yeah, I guess it could be the committee. Most of the class officers are there." Three of the four, anyway.

Layla laughed. "How would you know who the class officers were? Did you even go to school?"

"It was my freshman year when I skipped so much. Reggie took care of business once she found out, and I went to school religiously after that."

"Do you ever see your father now?" Layla asked, picking up on the fact that it was Reggie who'd yanked him back onto the straight and narrow, not his dad.

Justin gave a quick shake of his head. "No. We get the occasional call, and he pretends everything is normal. You know—a dad abandoning his teenage kids. Normal." Justin focused on the table for a moment. "He did support us, though."

"But he wasn't there enough," Layla said quietly.

Justin shook his head. "Nope. Can't say that he was. He'd promised no more long-haul truck jobs, but always took the next one that was offered."

The Smithwick's came and neither of them spoke as they both took a long, long draw.

Having the committee there was creeping him out to the point that he didn't mind talking about his father—mainly because of the one prominently missing member. Behind him chairs scraped against the floor just as a three-man band started to tune up, and a second later a hand clapped on to his shoulder.

"Hey, Justin. How fortuitous to run into you here. Did you get our letter?"

Justin looked up at a smiling David Heinz. "I did."

"Well, in addition to needing help on the committees, we're looking for a caterer for some of the reunion events and we have a very set budget. Any chance we could negotiate a price break?"

"Send me the info and I'll see what I can do." But he wasn't going to serve at his own reunion. He wasn't even going to be there.

"Great."

"You wouldn't happen to be in contact with Rachel, would you?" Paula Diaz asked.

Justin had half expected the question—after all, they'd dated and she'd been a class officer, so she should be in on the planning sessions, too. "No."

"None of us have. And the funny thing is we can't even get any cooperation from her parents." Paula shook her head in a mystified way. "Even though she moved just before graduation, we wanted her to come to the reunion."

"I tell you," David said, "she joined a cult. Couldn't face life after losing skater boy, here."

"I heard that was why she moved," Paula said. Justin's heart stalled out for a moment until she added, "Rumor had it her parents thought you were a bad influence." She waggled her eyebrows up and down in a humorous manner, making it obvious that she had no inkling of the truth.

Justin tried to smile. Truly he did. And then he changed the subject. "Just email the specs to the business and I'll get you the lowest price we can offer," he said, trying to get them the hell out of there. What did it mean that Rachel's parents wouldn't help them out?

It shouldn't bug him, but it did, although he could understand why Rachel wouldn't want to attend this reunion any more than he did.

His tactic had worked and Paula and David moved on. Justin looked up to see Layla quietly watching him. Try as he might, he could not bring himself totally back to the place he'd been before the committee had stopped by their table and blasted the shit out of his evening.

"Will you be attending your reunion?" Layla asked.

"No. Did you go to yours last year?"

"Helped plan it. I wasn't a class officer, but I was in town and people remembered me as being a workhorse."

"Did you enjoy yourself?"

"Not much. I was too busy worried about logistics and everything going smoothly." She smiled without humor. "I hope I can move past behaving like that."

She hadn't touched her beer other than that first draw, but instead sat with her hands in her lap. Justin took a long drink, met her eyes. Smiled.

Layla wasn't biting. "It bothers you that they can't find Rachel."

"I'm sure she's all right. Her parents weren't the most cooperative people in the world."

"Did you two date a long time?" Layla asked, tracing a path in the condensation on her glass, focusing on it rather than on him.

"Almost a year." The words came out clipped, and Layla looked up at him, probably wondering why a relationship that'd been over for more than ten years was making him respond like this. If their positions were reversed, he would have been wondering the same thing.

"Bitter breakup?"

"It's in the past, Layla." He reached across the table and took her hand, squeezed gently, but she didn't squeeze back.

CHAPTER EIGHT

LAYLA SAID NOTHING. What could she say? Perhaps she could make the observation that something was bothering the hell out of Justin and it was pretty obvious what it was.

Rachel.

Or the mention of her.

But Layla had enough Taylor in her to know not to push. Her gut said back off now, back off fast.

Justin was backing off even faster.

Time to put him out of his misery. Either that or spend a long, uncomfortable evening together. "You know, maybe we should call it a night. In all ways."

A look of sheer relief crossed his face. "I, uh—"

"It's been a strange evening. Not a good time to… Not a good time."

He nodded in agreement. A few minutes later he'd paid the tab and followed Layla past the dartboard and the Akita, out into the cool, early-evening air. They walked to his car without saying much, and he drove to her house a few silent minutes after that. He walked her to her door, dropped a kiss on her forehead.

"How chaste," she said.

He looked down at her and opened his mouth as if about to explain, but then closed it again. Instead he pulled her close and held her against him. She pressed her face to the soft corduroy of his jacket, inhaled and wondered what on earth was going on.

"Maybe we'll talk about all this sometime," he said when he stepped back a few seconds later, but Layla knew they wouldn't. Justin was a keeper of secrets. She'd always assumed he was an open book, but there was more to him. And somehow getting close to her threatened him.

"We're not going to go out again, are we?"

His expression didn't change, didn't

take on any hint of regret as he said, "No. I don't see that happening. But we will still be friends."

Layla nodded and opened her front door. She stepped inside and closed it without looking at him. Simply shut it in his face. And then she leaned back against the solid wood in her beautiful green dress and wondered where the evening had gone so wrong.

Could he have responded more transparently? Justin asked himself in disgust. Made it clearer that hearing about Rachel disturbed him?

No. There was something about Layla that made it harder to keep up the front. Probably because she'd known him for so long.

After dropping her off, Justin drove to the kitchen, parked in front and let himself in that way. Like all sane folk, he avoided back alleys after dark—even his own.

He shrugged out of the blazer and hung it in his locker, then went into his room and turned on the music. He'd get ahead of the game tonight, do as much of tomorrow's work as possible.

Justin pulled his stocking cap down to his ears.

The evening was unfortunate, but in some ways a godsend. Maybe Layla had had such a rotten time that she'd no longer be interested in seeing him in any capacity, and then he wouldn't be in danger of edging toward territory he had no intention of traveling through.

Maybe now they'd both go back to their own lives, hang with their own kind. Justin would find another party girl who understood just how temporary he was, and Layla could find a stable guy that wasn't an A-1 jerk.

LAYLA DECIDED THAT with the green dress she'd be just like Sam. Wear it once and discard it, because it reminded her of one of the strangest evenings she'd ever had.

Yes, she'd stood up to Robert and Melinda, and that had held a certain satisfaction. But nothing else had gone according

to plan. Even before the reunion committee had stopped by in the bar, the connection she'd felt with Justin up until tonight
had gone missing.

What had happened between the frosting kiss and this evening?

She was damned well going to find out,
because she didn't feel they were done yet.

THE NEXT TWO DAYS were crazy busy.
Justin got up at five o'clock to work on
the cakes he'd booked, then he drove up
to the lake to fill in for a vacationing chef,
arriving home around one in the morning
and then getting up four hours later. And
he welcomed the numbing exhaustion. Between the emotions Layla was stirring up
and the reunion committee looking high
and low for Rachel, he was doing way too
much thinking.

Eden and Reggie weren't helping—at
least not on the Layla front. Somehow
they'd gotten wind of the bust of a date.
Someone other than Robert and Melinda
and his graduating class officers must
have seen them out and about, and ratted

him out to his sisters. The only reason he knew was because Eden asked him if he'd enjoyed his date with Layla. He said yes, and left it at that.

Eden didn't. She didn't ask a lot of questions, but those she did ask were carefully planned and delivered in a nonchalant way. *What were Layla's plans for the future?* He didn't know. *Any chance that they might see her at their yearly summer picnic at the lake?* He didn't anticipate that happening. Finally…*are you still seeing Layla?* No. *Why?* Mind your own business, Eden.

She smiled with an odd sort of satisfaction when he snapped at her, as if she'd just figured something out. Well, he'd let her think that way all she wanted, as long as she left his private life alone.

His decision to back off fast from an entanglement with Layla, before any damage was done, had been a good one. He might have given her ego a knock during a vulnerable time, but better now than later.

The only problem was that if he wasn't thinking about her, he seemed to be thinking about his son, his speculations about the boy made worse by the almost ninety-nine percent guarantee that he'd never get answers.

Was he having such a hard time with this because his son was approaching his teen years, and Justin didn't know if he had someone to guide him through those turbulent times? He'd so wanted a father figure in his life back then, when the pain was still so raw from losing his mother. The one time he'd needed his dad, when he'd confessed that he was going to be a father, he was told that he'd made his bed and now had to lie in it.

Thanks, Dad. That was a lot of help for a frightened eighteen-year-old kid.

"Hey, Justin." Tammy Barnes, one of the waitresses who had just gotten off shift with him, sidled up as he unbuttoned his chef's jacket. "Want to get some coffee before you head down the mountain?"

He was so buzzed at the moment from a mixture of service-induced adrenaline—it had been a busy service for a Sunday night—and caffeine that he couldn't see having yet another cup.

"Maybe tomorrow," he said, folding the coat over his arm. He grabbed his jacket, then smiled at Tammy. "If I leave now, I may get an extra forty-five minutes sleep."

"You look done in," she said with a concerned expression.

"No more than usual," he assured her, suddenly having a very strong urge to yawn. He held it in until he turned his back and opened the door.

"Drive safe," she called, as he stepped outside and saw that the light rain had become sleet. There'd be no sleet in the Washoe Valley, but he'd have to keep his wits about him until he got below the freeze line.

He cranked the music up, cracked the window to get some air blowing over his face and pulled out onto the highway. He made this drive an average of three times a week, and sometimes the monotony got to him and his mind wandered.

When he hit age thirty, he'd quit the lake. Eighteen months to go. By that time, hopefully, he'd have the cake business established to the point that he didn't need the extra income from the hotel. The balloon payment would be made on his condo. From that point on, he'd go to Tahoe only to snowboard or play.

But again he was lying to himself. He worked to keep busy—to keep from having free time to be alone and think. His workaholic tendencies hadn't started until after culinary school, after he'd had the realization that his son was about to start first grade. About the time that pushing his guilt down deep had become more difficult.

Justin started up the summit, the sleet coming at him in mesmerizing streaks of white that the wipers swept away at the last minute. He was going to the kitchen late tomorrow. Maybe an hour late.

The car came up behind him fast, its lights flashing in his rearview mirror, causing a surge of adrenaline to jolt through him before it pulled out into the passing lane and zoomed by, traveling at too high a speed for road conditions.

Justin forced himself to loosen his death grip on the steering wheel as the other vehicle disappeared around a corner.

He swallowed drily. Shouldn't be any trouble staying awake now. Not with his heart knocking against his ribs.

Nobody's forcing you off the road tonight.

Like they had a year ago when he'd been mistakenly identified as a narc. His soon-to-be brother-in-law, Nick, a drug task force detective, had arrested the guy, who was now cooling his heels in prison, but the incident had left a mark.

Driving past the spot where the accident happened didn't bother Justin as much anymore, but headlights coming out of nowhere still triggered a reaction, one he was working on combating. Tonight he was kind of glad it had happened because maybe he'd get home without nodding off.

He cleared the summit and started down the other side, traveling even slower because of the accumulation of slushy snow on the road. Another vehicle came up behind him, but Justin had seen him miles ago. Being another invincible Californian in a four-wheel drive truck, the guy sailed by, signaling to pull back into Justin's lane. Only it didn't exactly work out as planned. The bed end of the truck, which had no weight to speak of, started to drift to the left on the slick road as the driver attempted to pull in.

"Hold on, buddy," Justin muttered, tapping his brakes, trying desperately to keep some distance between them. They were almost at the place where he'd been forced off the road. Surely this couldn't happen twice....

Oh, it was happening.

The truck went into a sideways skid, smashing into the guardrail in front of Justin, then bouncing back off, the front wheels catching the edge of the pavement and flipping the four-wheel drive onto its side seconds before the Challenger also went into a skid and rammed into the rear bumper.

The two vehicles slid to a stop in tandem. Justin, fearful of other traffic coming around the curve and slamming into them, flipped open his cell and dialed the National Highway Patrol with his thumb as he went to check the other driver. No need.

"Son of a bitch!" the guy yelled as he pushed open the passenger door of his truck like the hatch on a submarine and climbed out. He walked over and kicked one of the tires.

Justin took a few steps back. Probably best not to engage him. He appeared uninjured, but was tottering on the brink of losing it.

The dispatcher came on the line and Justin reported the accident, then went back to his car for the road flares he kept in his trunk. It wasn't the first time he'd used them to mark an accident on the grade, but it was the first time since the wreck last year that his car had been involved.

The other driver was pacing in the snow around the truck, ranting, kicking slush, flailing his arms, so Justin leaned back against the guardrail several yards away after lighting the flares, and calculated the cost of putting a new front end on his car.

He hoped this ranting guy with the big-ass four-wheel drive had insurance. And he hoped his sisters didn't ride him about this, because it wasn't even close to his fault.

He also hoped his life started easing back to its normal path.

Since agreeing to give Layla a ride home, he'd gotten a black eye, broken into a school and wrecked his car. And somehow he had a feeling that his run of questionable luck wasn't over yet.

"HEY, LAYLA?" Sam called from the back room of her shop. "Your phone is ringing in your purse." A second later, as Layla pushed the beaded curtains aside, Sam said, "Layla's phone. Yes. She's right here."

She held out the cell, and when Layla answered, she found herself slightly breathless. Justin, maybe? Very few people called her.

"Hi, Layla. Dillon Conrad."

Good grief. What now? "Hello, Dillon," she said cautiously, wondering why the guy who taught science down the hall from her room could possibly be calling. Had they figured out that she and Justin had taken her lessons? And if they did, then what?

"I'm calling you on the q.t. Have you gotten an invitation to the Merit Awards?"

"No."

"I didn't think so. When Ella gave me my invitation, I saw an invitation clearly addressed to you in care of the school sitting on her desk. I don't think it's right if she doesn't inform you of it."

"Thank you."

"Not that you'd want to go, but you've won another award and you deserve it." There was a brief, uncomfortable pause and then he said, "Are you doing all right? Is there anything Judy or I could do? If you need a recommendation or something..."

"Actually, I'm going back to school."

"Hey, that's great to hear."

"Yes."

After another silence, he said, "Well, I'll let you go."

"Thanks for calling. I truly appreciate it." And she also appreciated knowing she had a friend. No one else from the school had contacted her since she'd left. She hadn't been ultraclose to any of the other teachers, but they had socialized on occasion. Apparently, there would be no more of that.

When Layla shut off her phone, she turned to see her sister waiting expectantly to hear the details.

"I won an award," she said with a slight shrug, making a mental note never to take a call of a truly personal nature in the shop. Sam was one of those people who tended to keep her own affairs a mystery, but fully expected to share in every part of Layla's life.

"Educational?"

"What else?" A nice bit of irony. Layla leaned her arms on the counter between them.

Her sister laughed. "That should stick in that bitch principal's craw."

Layla smiled as she clasped her hands loosely together. "There is one small problem, though. My invitation is at the school. I don't think the principal is going to tell me about it."

Sam's eyes, which already looked huge due to the false lashes she wore, went even wider. "If you want to go get it, I'll come with you." She made a grab for her purse. "We can go right now."

As satisfying as that mental picture was—showing up at school with her unconventional sister ready to go to bat for her—it would probably result in a trespassing charge or something.

Layla had an easier solution. "I'll call the Merit Awards office and RSVP by phone. Then I'll show up at the ceremony."

"Alone?"

"Not necessarily. You could come."

"But if you needed an actual date, Willie—"

Layla's eyes shot to Sam's face. "No."

"But—"

"Sam, your friend hums when he's

bored, and this ceremony will be very boring to someone not winning an award."

"Perhaps he's over that."

"He wasn't the last time we went out." A date that Sam had arranged a year ago, just prior to Layla meeting Robert.

"Did he hum *a lot?*" As if a small amount of humming during a boring educational award ceremony would be acceptable.

Layla nodded. They'd gone to an art gallery opening and Willie had been okay in the beginning, but by the end her elbow was sore from nudging him. "His favorite tune was 'Yellow Submarine.'"

Sam gave a resigned nod. "That sounds like Willie."

"He's a nice guy," Layla said in a placating tone.

"No. It's fine. Really. I'd just like to see him settled."

"But not with me, okay?"

"Okay." Sam picked up the steamer and started working over a filmy silk robe, humming "Yellow Submarine" lightly under her breath.

Sometimes Layla envied her sister's ability to simply let matters drop and move on. If Layla had that ability herself, she probably wouldn't have wasted so much time obsessing over matters she couldn't control.

She was learning, though. For instance, she was dealing with her cheating boyfriend and being fired better than she'd ever thought possible. And she knew why: she was distracted by other matters.

Had it not been for Justin, and her realization that she found him ridiculously attractive, she would have been obsessing about her career a whole lot more. Instead, she was wondering why, when there was so obviously good chemistry between them, Justin was taking a giant step back just as she was ready to take a giant step forward.

She looked at her sister. "Tell me about Rachel Kelly."

Sam turned, the steamer blowing a cloud of condensation into the air as she pulled it away from the robe. "Rachel?"

"You know. Justin's old high school

girlfriend. The person who helped you get through government class."

Sam gave a casual shrug. Too casual. "Not much to tell," she said, going back to the robe, which was totally wrinkle free. "She had rich parents who wanted her to be one way. She wanted to be another. The parents won."

"She moved before graduation?"

Sam hesitated, then nodded and started steaming the robe again.

"How many times are you going to de-wrinkle that one robe?"

"Until I get it right," Sam muttered.

"What do you know about Rachel?"

Her sister turned then. "I don't know anything about a girl who disappeared from my life ten years ago. Anything else?"

"Was she pregnant?" Layla spoke almost before the pieces had fully clicked into place—Justin's behavior with the re-union committee, Rachel's disappearance from school months before graduation. But once they did click, it made perfect sense.

Sam lifted her chin. "I can honestly say I don't know."

Layla believed her. "Did you suspect?"

"All I can tell you is that Rachel withdrew into herself for a couple months, barely talked to me in class, and then, boom. Gone."

Layla nodded.

"Even if she was pregnant, what does it matter?" Sam asked.

Layla pushed her hair back from her temples, wondering the exact same thing. "It doesn't, I guess." Although it would explain a few things for her.

Sam came around the counter. "Justin is hot. But he's also a player. He is not going to settle down. Don't try to figure him out. Don't try to fix him."

She hated that her sister could read her so easily. Layla was the Taylor who made the observations and attempted to direct her errant siblings down the correct path in life. Not that they ever followed her advice…just as she wasn't going to follow Sam's. "What makes you think I want to settle down or fix him?"

Sam's expression took on a sad cast.

"Because that's the way you are. You like stability. You want everyone else to be stable." She reached out and squeezed Layla's shoulder. "Some of us aren't."

"SO YOU'RE REALLY all right? As in unscathed?" Eden spoke in a low, disbelieving voice.

"Damn it, Eden, it was the car that got creamed. Not me." Justin paced through the empty kitchen, the phone at his ear.

"But it *could* have been you."

This was what he got for apprising his sister of the situation rather that just dealing with it. Except that now he needed her driveway to work on the car, so she would have figured out what'd happened anyway. Eden tended to notice things like a vehicle with a smashed-in hood sitting in front of her garage.

As if he had time for this. Patty's last day was tomorrow—Tuesday—and after that he'd be buried in work.

"But it wasn't me," he said for the third time.

"Are you sure you can't afford to quit at

the lake?" They'd had this same conversation after his last accident. Only Reggie had been there with Eden, double-teaming him.

"After the big payment on the condo, I can quit."

"That's more than a year away."

"It'll take me that long to save the money."

Eden made a growling noise on the other end of the phone, probably because she couldn't yell at him while serving a luncheon. He called her only because he wanted her to know what had happened the night before, and why he was borrowing her SUV, parked at the kitchen, to deliver a cake. His second car, a small Honda, wasn't up to the task of hauling that many layers.

He should have left a note.

"I can't help it if I bought the condo at the wrong time." Just before the housing market had gone to hell. His timing was always impeccable. Now he was upside down and had no choice but to surge on. The problem with being a small-business owner was that the income was not always steady.

"But maybe you could get a job locally."

"Not one that pays like this one."

Another growl. "Be careful with my vehicle!"

"I will. And thanks."

"We're not through."

"Yes, we are."

He finished loading the cake tiers into the SUV and securing the boxes so they didn't move during the trip down to Carson City. After setting up the cake, he'd head on up to the lake for his last shift of the week, and hopefully avoid asshole drivers who thought four-wheel drive gave them the ability to speed regardless of conditions.

His fault or not, Eden would kill him if he wrecked her SUV.

CHAPTER NINE

LAYLA WENT HOME from Sunshine of Your Love shortly after the Rachel discussion, more irritated than she wanted to acknowledge about Sam lecturing her.

Sam. Lecturing her.

And Layla couldn't stop thinking about Rachel Kelly.

If she had been pregnant, it wasn't necessarily with Justin's child. He'd dated her during their senior year, but had he been her only partner? People that age were known to cheat…hell, people of any age cheated. Like, say, Robert.

Layla grabbed the usual handful of junk mail from her box and dug her key out of her jacket pocket just as her phone rang. She let it ring while she opened the door and put down the mail. The phone went silent, then a few seconds later started ringing again.

Her mother or Sam. The persistent people in her life. Layla checked the number before answering.

Her mother. Whom she hadn't called after being fired. She should have, but it wasn't something she wanted to discuss with her mom. Losing her job was embarrassing—especially when she was the responsible child. It was as if everything she'd stood for had been proved wrong.

Wait—she'd already figured that out. Everything she'd stood for *was* wrong. Perhaps she and her mother would have more common ground now that she was no longer the only Taylor child who hadn't been fired or gone bankrupt.

"Mom, hi."

"Hello, Layla love."

It felt good to hear her voice.

"I'm surprised I haven't heard from you sooner," Layla admitted. "Sam said she told you what happened."

"I thought that it'd be best to wait a few days, give us both some time to get our heads together." Her mom's tone sounded off. Stilted.

"I appreciate that."

"Then why on earth are you thinking about quitting your job?"

Quitting her job? Crap. Sam had obviously done some damage control for her. Wonderful. It'd be easier to simply go with Sam's version, but Layla couldn't bring herself to lie to her parent. Or anyone else, for that matter.

"I didn't exactly quit. I was asked to transfer back to Life Skills and chose to resign instead." Okay, she could lie to her parent. She simply couldn't bring herself to confess that she'd been fired. The word still made a knot form in her stomach.

"You've *already* resigned? As in fait accompli?"

Layla sawllowed, feeling shifty and hating it. "Yes."

"So now I have only one question," her mother said blandly, before her voice sharpened. "Are you really my eldest daughter? And if not, what have you done with her?"

How was Layla supposed to take that?

"Yes, I am your eldest," she finally said in a flat tone. "I thought you would be happy I'm trying to stretch my wings. Discover myself." Not exactly true, but this was language her parents, children of the seventies, understood.

"Layla, honey, you don't have a good base for wing stretching. If you did, you'd have done it years ago."

"What?" she demanded, outraged.

"It's not in your nature to do things like this. Your father and I have discussed the matter, several times in fact, and we agree. Sam says you don't even have a major. This is very out of character."

"I disagree."

"Honey, I think I know your character. You were color coding your clothes when you were four. Reds and pinks in the top drawer—"

"I remember," Layla said. And there was nothing wrong with a child organizing her clothing. It helped her find what she wanted. It did not mean that she wanted to color code every part of her life.

"So the job is really over. You currently have no means of support."

"I'm going to graduate school and I have Grandma Bonnie's inheritance, which, if you recall, she asked in her will that we spend."

There was a very long silence. "You've never in your life spent rainy day money."

"Maybe I've never seen rain," Layla countered.

"And what's this about dating Justin?"

"What?" Sam must have been on the phone within seconds of her leaving the shop. Her mother was trying to help; Layla knew that. She was also confusing the heck out of her.

"I went out with him a couple of times."

"But Justin… Remember how angry he used to make you?"

The key phrase being "used to." Now he turned her on.

"I thought you loved Justin."

"I do. He was practically a son…but he is so not right for you."

"It's not like I want to marry him." And then Layla realized one very important fact. As much as she still craved parental approval, she was thirty blinking years old and could make her own decisions—concerning her job, her future and the men she dated.

"People change, Mom. I have."

"I'm just concerned about too much change in too short a time."

"What would be the proper length of time?"

"I, uh…"

Her mother trailed off and Layla said, "I'm fine. Taking good care of myself, and Sam will report back if I do anything foolish. I love you, but I have to go. Goodbye, Mom."

There was a pause, and then her mother said, "Do not make any rash decisions!" just as Layla hung up the phone.

Sheesh.

Talk about a strange and depressing call. Her mom had no faith in her ability to survive without a nine-to-five job and a man in her life who wore a suit and tie. Her siblings seemed fine during their occasional spells of unemployment and sofa surfing and dating questionable people, but her parents had no faith in Layla's ability to do the same. And she was the oldest. Way too old to be thinking *I'll show them,* but those exact words were being etched into her mind, and it took some effort to stop the process.

She couldn't really blame people for expecting her to act as she always had. But she wasn't the same person she'd been even a month ago, and they'd better get used to that.

BY THE TIME EDEN returned from service, Justin was once again in his pastry room, piping filling into éclairs.

"The cake delivery went well?" she asked as she leaned against the doorjamb.

"Did you see any dents on your vehicle?" Justin asked without looking up.

"None that I didn't put there myself." She'd checked. He'd known she would. Anything for ammo. Eden shifted slightly. "I've been driving you crazy and I apologize."

Justin glanced up, his eyebrows raised. "Is this reverse psychology?"

Eden brushed the hair away from her temple. "This is your sister asking you to slow down."

Justin nodded.

"But you're not going to, are you?"

He started piping again. "I'm giving your suggestions some deep thought."

He heard her inhale sharply, waited for the explosion, but it didn't come. And he didn't dare look at her, for fear of triggering it.

Finally, Eden said, "I don't care how you live your life as long as it doesn't affect business."

"I appreciate that."

"You need to slow down."

"I will."

"Liar."

He glanced up at her and smiled. "I've not even thirty. I can handle this."

"Then maybe you can handle telling me what the hell is bugging you?"

He tried to hold the smile, but failed.

Something about a deep emotional jab to his midsection.

"Whatever is bugging me—and I'm not saying something is bugging me—will not affect business. And if something bugs me in the future I won't let it affect business. I never have and I never will. Okay?"

Eden raised her hands in surrender. "Fine." She backed out of the room without another word, leaving Justin with a decidedly unsettled feeling.

It wasn't like Eden to suddenly give up. But maybe she was finally starting to get it through her head that Justin was under no obligation to share.

THIS WAS IT. Zero hour. The worst Justin could do was reject her again.

Even so, Layla pulled open the door to Tremont Catering with more confidence than she felt. After the phone call with her mother the previous day, and more than an hour with a UNR advisor today discussing the merits of a straight education masters versus one in another field, such as psychology, only one thing was certain—absolutely nothing. And that was the attitude Layla had when she walked into the kitchen. Nothing was certain. She could live with that. She hoped.

Recent events had taught her that even if you played by the rules, unexpected circumstances could swamp your life, change its direction forever. And reconnect you with a guy from your past that you'd never dreamed you wanted to be reconnected with.

Surely there had to be a reason for that?

"Hello?" she called as she stood in the empty waiting area. The door to the kitchen was propped open with a cast-iron Eiffel Tower.

Layla heard footsteps in response to her call. Light footsteps, not Justin's heavier tread. Oh, well.

She was nervous, so she smiled her teacher smile when Eden came around the corner, her blond hair pulled up into a messy knot that suited her cheerleader good looks. Layla had always wished her hair would cooperate with knots and rubber bands, but it didn't. She had one hairdo and she was wearing it. Fine, dark hair with a slight wave brushing her shoulders.

"Layla?"

Eden actually sounded friendly. That was a plus. The two of them had graduated from the same high school the same year, but despite having brothers who were practically joined at the hip, had never found a comfortable ground on which to build a friendship, perhaps because their social lives were polar opposites. Eden had been the perky, popular cheerleader, while Layla hid out in the library, held office in the Honor Society and belonged to several small clubs with the other shy, studious kids.

Loserville, in the teen way of seeing things, but she'd never felt like a loser. Just impatient for high school to be over so she could get on with her life, follow her plans. Show those popular kids what a serious student could accomplish in the real world, away from the cliques and popularity contests.

That hadn't worked out too well for her of late.

"Hi, Eden. I, uh…is Justin here?"

Exactly what was she going to say if he was? Layla straightened her back. She was going to ask him out. Again. And when he said no, she was going to ask him why not. At the very least she figured he'd want to discuss matters privately rather than here at the kitchen, and would agree to set something up.

That was the master plan, anyway. She'd refused to let herself practice the words. She was going to wing it…when she got the chance.

"No. He won't be in until tomorrow."

Layla felt a huge rush of disappointment mixed with relief.

Eden cocked her head. "Did you leave something else in his car?"

She smiled again, knowing it probably came off as a grimace. "No. I just wanted to see him."

"Anything I can help you with?" his sister asked, obviously fishing.

"I don't think so. It doesn't involve the

kitchen." Layla didn't mean to sound mysterious, but she was hardly going to say, "I just want to proposition your brother." Nope. Couldn't see doing that.

Eden slowly nodded her head, her fingertips resting lightly on the counter in front of her, a flashy engagement ring catching the light on her left hand. "Forgive me for saying this, but it's kind of strange having you and Justin—" she gestured as she searched for words "—in contact."

"Kind of like worlds colliding?"

The corners of Eden's mouth tilted up. Surprise, no doubt, that Layla was showing a bit of spunk instead of clamming up as she usually did when things got personal. "Exactly."

"I don't know about Justin's world, but I can tell you that lately mine has been, well, bizarre."

"How so?"

"It started when Justin walked into that bar at Lake Tahoe to rescue me. Then that photo of me throwing up went viral through the student community, and I ended up getting fired."

Eden looked totally confused. "Fired?"

So Justin had kept his mouth shut. Points to him.

His sister leaned her elbows on the counter and clasped her hands together, the diamond on her ring again catching the light. Layla wondered if she was engaged to someone she knew. "*You* got fired?" Eden asked.

Layla debated for a second—keeping her dignity had always been her first and foremost concern—then figured what the hell, and poured out the story of exactly what had happened to her after Robert's bombshell. It had to get easier with each telling, didn't it?

Eden listened with rapt attention, her mouth dropping open a couple times. "Does your boss know about Robert and Melinda?" she interrupted at one point to ask.

"I told her." And now maybe Ella would look at perfect Melinda differently.

"So what are you going to do?" Eden

asked, and Layla realized this was a) the longest she'd probably ever talked to Justin's sister and b) kind of fun. Perhaps she'd been intimidated by the cheerleader image and all that went with it for too long—like a dozen years too long.

And maybe she'd been resentful that the boys, Justin, Derek and Eric, had never bothered Eden or Reggie. Only her. The reactive one. Eden had been too cute and Reggie too scary.

"I'm starting classes in June."

"Master's degree in education?"

Layla rubbed a hand over the side of her neck. "That's one possibility, but nothing is carved in stone at the moment."

Eden stared at her and Layla knew exactly what she was thinking. Layla Taylor without a definite plan. Pigs must be flying.

Or at least she thought she knew what Eden was thinking. She was proved wrong when Justin's sister said, "So what will you do until classes start?"

"I'm formatting some lessons for self-publication." Although, other than organizing the papers into piles, she had yet to begin. It was a big, big job.

"Is there a deadline for that?"

Layla shook her head. "Only a self-imposed one."

Eden narrowed her eyes in an appraising way. "Justin told you that our prep cook is having surgery, didn't he?"

"Yes," Layla said. "He did mention that."

"And offered you the job in the midst of a drunken episode?"

"He did." Did Justin's sister know he'd kissed her? That she'd kissed him back? Several times? Had she figured out that was why Layla was here?

"Do you want to do it? She'll be back before your classes start."

Layla's pulse leaped. "I'm not that experienced in the kitchen. Just home economics type stuff." A class she'd aced, but still...

Eden leaned more heavily on her forearms. "All it involves is keeping Justin out of the weeds."

"Excuse me?"

"He's burning the candle at both ends and doing his best to ignite the middle. Patty, our prep cook, has been carrying a lot of his load, and without her…" Eden made a downward spiraling motion with her index finger as she gave a low whistle.

"Why is he doing that?" Layla had been wondering, and truly wanted to know why a guy who'd been so carefree as a kid was now working such a ridiculous schedule.

Eden met her eyes candidly. "He says it's because of the condo payments, but he's been like this since culinary school. And it's been getting worse lately. He was in a car accident on the mountain Sunday evening—"

Layla's musing as to whether or not this was because he'd fathered a child stopped dead. "Is he all right?" she blurted, before realizing that if he wasn't, Eden wouldn't be calmly hiring an assistant for him.

"According to Justin, he is. Just a slippery road, but I don't know…. I want him to get some sleep while Patty is out, and he needs help. We all need help. I was about to hire a temp, but…" Eden shifted her jaw sideways in an appraising way. "Want to give it a go for a couple days? See if it works out?"

"So I would just follow directions?" Layla asked.

"That's all. It's like chemistry lab. Remember chemistry lab with Crabby Abby?"

Mrs. Abigail. Oh, yes. Layla remembered.

She'd been the queen of chemistry lab, Crabby Abby's pet student, and Eden, who'd been in the same lab, had been famous for screwing up every single experiment. Of course, guys came out of the woodwork to help her.

"I can handle that. But—" she cleared her throat "—I know there must be a lot of people with more experience than me who'd love a shot at cooking here for a few weeks."

Eden gave her a very candid look. "Honestly? Justin needs someone like you around."

"Excuse me?"

"You won't put up with his bull and, well, I think you'd be good for him."

Layla's bag slipped off her shoulder, but she caught the strap before it hit the floor. "Are you setting us up?" Egads.

Eden leaned closer. "I'm trying to knock some sense into my hardheaded brother before he has a meltdown and we have to go looking for a new dessert chef."

"How will hiring me help?"

"You guys have known each other forever. You're steady. Stable. And frankly, I think he likes you."

"You want me to be a calming influence?"

Eden laughed. "I want you to help double-team him."

CHAPTER TEN

"YOU HIRED LAYLA?" Justin slapped his white cotton stocking cap on his thigh, then pulled it over his hair in preparation for doing battle with one monster of a wedding cake, trying hard not to look either angry or disturbed. "Why?"

"It was originally your idea," Eden pointed out.

"I was drunk."

"Maybe you shouldn't get that drunk."

"I don't do it often." And he'd had a reason for that particular binge. "I thought we made hiring decisions as a team."

"You weren't available!" Eden stood with her hand on her hip, the position she assumed whenever she was taking control—which had started when he'd been a toddler and she'd announced that she was the boss. "And I didn't think you'd mind since, *again,* it was your idea."

He opened his mouth, then thought better of it. Arguing would only spur her on. Unfortunately, not arguing had the same effect.

"You need help," Eden said, dropping her hands to her sides and leaning forward, jutting her chin out for emphasis. "You've been in two car accidents driving home from Tahoe. At least now you can get some more sleep."

"Sleep had nothing to do with those car accidents, and one of them was attempted murder."

"How close have you come to falling asleep at the wheel on your many drives off the mountain?" Eden demanded.

Justin shifted his weight. "I've never fallen asleep."

"Have you come close?"

He didn't answer immediately, and she pounced. "That precludes any veto power you have over my decision to get help during the time that Patty is out."

"I've never had a problem with you

hiring help," Justin said. "Actual cooking help, that is. But Layla?" What was up with that? Was his sister setting him up… with someone stable? Please, not that.

"You should have seen her in chemistry class," Eden continued.

"*Chemistry* class?"

Eden adjusted the lapels of her chef's coat. "She starts tomorrow."

Justin shook his head and then stalked across the kitchen to his locker. He slammed his small gym bag, containing the clean black pants he'd change into to help cater a party that afternoon, into it.

This was not the way the world was supposed to work. Or it wasn't the way it had worked for the past twenty-eight years.

"It isn't forever," Eden called across the kitchen as she diced carrots with a vengeance. "If Reggie can hold out until her due date, and Patty comes back early, then we'll get by. If not, we'll hire a temp for a couple weeks."

"Yeah, yeah, yeah," he said as he closed

his locker. "But maybe we should have gotten a real temp."

"Or maybe you can quit your job at the lake and we won't need a temp."

We've been over that.

He went into the pastry room and closed the door, even though he didn't need to in order to make the batter for mini cupcakes. He simply wanted time to think, to figure out why having Layla there seemed like such a threat.

Maybe because he had no idea why she would agree to such a thing.

What was her objective? Layla never did anything without having an objective.

Shit. Maybe *he* was her objective.

But he hadn't heard from her in days, not since the rotten date, and now this. Frankly, the whole Layla situation was confusing the hell out of him.

SAM'S STORE WAS PACKED with sorority girls when Layla stopped by near closing. She went into the back and started unpacking newly arrived lingerie while she waited for Sam to ring up the final sales and close up shop.

"I'm working part-time at Tremont Catering starting tomorrow," Layla called through the beaded curtains after her sister had escorted the last customer to the door and locked the dead bolt.

Sam instantly appeared in the doorway, pushing back the strands of purple beads. "Get out."

"It's true. Their prep cook is having surgery."

"Did Justin hire you?" Sam asked darkly, releasing the beads as she walked on into the room.

"Nope," Layla said lightly, taking a red bra out of its protective plastic bag. "Eden." Layla still wasn't clear on the double-teaming.

"None of this makes sense." Sam leaned back against the counter. "Do you have enough cooking know-how to help in a professional kitchen?"

"I know how to cook, and Eden says I'll be following directions."

"You do excel at that," Sam said drily.

Indeed. At Christmastime she was the Taylor who spent the entire day working on all the gifts that required assembly, because she was the only one who would actually read the directions instead of diving in, opening packets and jamming various components together.

"Are you calling Mom tonight?"

Sam thoughtfully pushed a few strands of bright red hair behind her ears. "No. I don't think I'll do that."

"Thank you." Layla pulled another red package out of the shipping box. "Any more questions or comments? Because I assure you I have answers." Or at least a pretty good bluff.

"I just…nothing. Congratulations." Sam gave a slight cough. "Will you still be available here for the occasional afternoon?"

"I wouldn't miss it," Layla replied, holding up the red panties she'd just unwrapped—panties that seemed to be missing the crotch. "I've really broadened my horizons since working here."

THE METAL DOOR to the kitchen was once again wedged open when Layla entered Tremont Catering at exactly 7:00 a.m. She heard low voices and followed them into the kitchen, where Justin and an obviously pregnant Reggie were conferring over several sheets of paper spread across the counter.

Layla paused in the doorway, glancing around at the stark work area, all stainless steel and tile, the only color being Reggie's red smock. Even Justin was dressed entirely in neutrals.

"Morning," she said, her voice sounding unnaturally bright. *Nerves.*

Reggie smiled and Layla noted that somehow Justin's oldest sister managed to look elegant and put together despite the bump under her smock top. Layla felt positively frumpy by comparison in her cream-colored scoop-neck T-shirt and slim khaki pants, although she did fit nicely into the neutral color scheme.

"How long's it been?" Reggie asked. "Ten years?"

"At least," Layla replied. Reggie had left

for culinary school around the same time she and Eden had graduated from high school, leaving Justin to fend for himself that last year. Not that she and Reggie were more than nodding acquaintances. They'd both kept to themselves back then, and frankly, Reggie had always intimidated Layla. She'd seemed so…perfect. Pretty much the antithesis of her brother.

"We're glad you're here," Reggie said, apparently speaking for both of them, since Justin had yet to say anything. If they'd been closer, Layla wouldn't have been surprised to see Reggie elbow her brother in the ribs to get a response out of him. As it was, she said, "Aren't we?"

Justin gave a silent nod.

He was not taking the invasion well, and Layla was feeling just stubborn enough not to let it bother her. He'd made her crazy as a child. Turnabout was fair. In fact, it was rather satisfying. And even more satisfying because no one—not her mother or her sister, or her former nemesis—seemed to think she could do anything outside the box, such as take a job for the hell of it.

"We're just plotting out the desserts for the rest of the week, so you may as well come over and see what you'll be helping with."

Layla crossed to the counter, standing on the opposite side from Justin, while Reggie explained the various functions they were catering that week. When she finally glanced up at him, after Reggie had finished, there was no laughter in his eyes, no sense of a plot about to hatch. He looked amazingly serious.

"So," Reggie said, settling a hand on top of her baby bump, "I'll go to work on kabobs and you two can work on the desserts."

"Sounds good," Justin said. He gestured with his head to where he worked on the cakes, and Layla followed.

As soon as she was in the room, which was several degrees cooler than the main kitchen, he closed the door. And still he did not smile.

"Why are you here?" he asked mildly.

"This was originally your idea."

He gave her a look that told her this wasn't the first time he'd heard that, and it occurred to her that since they'd reconnected, she held as much power as he did. The dynamic had shifted. Before, as kids, they had played by Justin's rules—he was the offense and she was defense. Possession never changed.

It had today.

Layla placed her palm on the marble slab sitting on the counter, testing the surface. It felt remarkably cool—either that or she was remarkably warm. "I stopped by the kitchen and Eden asked me if I wanted to fill in until your prep cook was back on her feet."

He scowled at her, but there was something in his expression that made her much more aware of him, of herself, than she had been a few seconds before. "Why'd you take the job?"

"I'm looking for something different in my life."

"Catering experience?" he asked in a

soft voice that sent a tingle skittering up her spine.

She walked a few steps until she was kitty-corner across the stainless-steel counter from him. "That along with other things." Amazing how she could speak so calmly with her heart in her throat.

His mouth twisted, but other than that, no reaction. Perhaps he was hoping she'd back down if he was quiet long enough.

Fat chance. She'd been photographed throwing up in a bush. Her boyfriend had admitted to sleeping around on her because she was a tight-ass. She was no stranger to humiliation.

Justin shook his head. "Not a great idea."

"For you or for me?"

"Both of us."

"Why?"

"Because—" he set his palms on the counter and leaned toward her, close enough that she could smell cedar soap "—I'm not much for longevity and you have longevity written all over you."

Layla laughed. "Then you're reading

things wrong. You and me? Longevity? Justin, I just wanted to have some fun."

"Fun. Just fun."

He didn't believe her. She wasn't certain she believed herself, but she had a point to make. She let out an audible breath that sounded too much like a discouraged sigh.

"Have you ever used the words *tight* and *ass* in the same sentence as my name?" she asked.

"You know I have," he said, a humorless smile curving his lips.

"Well, so did Robert."

The smile disappeared. "Robert is an asshole."

"He has a few good qualities or I wouldn't have dated him. Although," she allowed, "not many come to mind right now."

"Layla, I'm flattered that you want to have me as your rebound guy—"

Her eyes flashed. "I'm not trying to flatter you. I thought we had some chemistry and it's a shame not to act on it. No longevity involved, unless it's a mutual feeling. Damn it, I trust you, crazy as it sounds."

"It does sound crazy."

"Crazy or not, relationships don't seem to be working for me just now. My career has taken a nasty downturn. I'm rethinking my life and I wouldn't mind experiencing a few new things while I do that."

"So the kitchen is one of those new experiences?"

"Yes."

"And I'm another?" He moved closer to her, close enough that she could feel the heat of his body, once again smell the cedar-scented soap he used, and suddenly she had the feeling she was slipping in over her head. So she casually shrugged her shoulders instead of answering.

"Layla, just because we kissed a few times and it was good…"

"What?" she asked. "It doesn't mean you're interested in me? Fine. I can handle that." Layla was so very glad that she had years of experience dealing with him in other ways, or she'd be a pool of humiliation spreading across the tile floor. "But

I'm staying here until Eden tells me I'm fired." One corner of her mouth tipped up into a careless half smile. "I'll bet getting fired the second time is even easier than the first."

A weary and wary expression crossed Justin's face. "What do you want from me, Layla?"

"I think I just laid that out, then you told me it wasn't going to happen, and now I'm done talking."

But I'm not going home.

His lips twisted slightly and then he opened the door to the kitchen. "I have to get to work."

"Meaning…?"

"There are aprons folded on the shelf next to the lockers by the back door. Go get one."

"Conversation over?"

"As if it never happened."

JUSTIN FELT RIDICULOUSLY off center, although he'd rather take a beating than admit it. Layla had laid out her position with remarkable aplomb. She wanted to loosen up, and had chosen him to help her out. It was all very tidy and planned out and Layla-esque; pretty much the opposite of what she said she wanted.

He wasn't biting.

The logical part of his brain told him that if she truly meant what she said, there would be no problem. A few dates, a few good times, then they'd move on to their separate lives. His gut, on the other hand, was sending out danger signals. This was Layla. Yeah, he could see having a fling with her, but he honestly didn't know if he could walk away unscathed. And what if she, heaven forbid, started taking things seriously?

He didn't want to hurt Layla and he probably would.

Robert had hurt her, and she was looking for something new, maybe to boost her ego, maybe for a touch of revenge...but she was also vulnerable. And he'd known her long enough to feel protective. So here he was, protecting both of them, because he wasn't exactly in a good place himself, and Layla was anything but appreciative.

Her cheeks were faintly pink when she came back with the apron, but it was from anger, not self-consciousness. He recognized the spark in her eye—the same one he'd put there many times years ago with his pranks. However, she'd never fought back like this. She usually said something that was both lofty and cutting and then retreated. This time there was no retreat. It unnerved him.

"The recipes are here," he said abruptly, opening a drawer and pulling out a stack of plastic coated cards strung on a loose-leaf binder ring. He flipped through them. "Cakes are on the yellow cards. Fillings, blue. Frostings and icings, pink."

"Nice system."

"I have my moments." He handed her the cards. "We're making lemon today. Come on, I'll show you where we keep everything."

He led her through the kitchen to the walk-in and the dry storage area, pointing out where everything was while he gathered eggs, butter, lemons. The dry ingredients he used frequently were stored in a cabinet in the pastry room. He opened the door once he'd deposited the items he'd picked up onto the counter next to the mixer.

"Get the flour, salt, sugar and baking powder."

It took Layla a few minutes to find everything, but she did, making several trips. When Patty had started, she'd moved slowly, too, so he tamped down his impatience, which was probably more a result of circumstances. In the end, showing Layla what to do wouldn't take much more time than doing it all himself.

"Okay, first you cream a pound of butter," he said, unwrapping a one pound brick and chopping it into chunks before starting the mixer and dropping them in. "Let this run for about five minutes. We want a lot of air in the butter…."

Layla was, as he'd assumed, a quick study, but she still took notes in a small book she'd pulled from her rear jeans pocket. She'd probably been taking notes since she'd first learned to write.

Patty had taken notes, too.

In fact, Layla and Patty were quite similar in that regard, but Patty didn't make him feel protective or defensive. Or, heaven help him, attracted to her.

How could he possibly be both defensive and lustful? Maybe because he'd never seen this side of Layla before?

After showing her how to prepare the cake pans and pour the batter, he started on the pastry dough for the mini tartlets to be served that afternoon at a late luncheon Eden and Reggie were catering.

"When will you frost the cake?" Layla asked. She was all business, but again, he saw the glint of battle in her eye.

"I'll start tomorrow," he said. He glanced up at her from where he rolled out dough. "Have you ever done any cake decorating?"

She shook her head. "How about I do that?" She pointed at the pastry dough.

"Sure," he said. If she rolled crusts, then he could start the filling.

"How thick?"

"A sixteenth. No thicker." Her eyes narrowed as she mentally estimated. "Like this," he muttered, then tore off a corner of the dough and held it up for her to see. "Just take one of those balls of dough, flour that marble board and start rolling. If the dough sticks, flour the rolling pin. Don't overwork it."

"Got it," Layla said. She took a handful of flour and masterfully tossed it onto the board, spreading it with a quick swipe of her palm. She seemed totally at home with the process.

"Do you bake much?" he asked.

"No," she answered blandly. "But I got an A in home economics."

AFTER JUSTIN DISAPPEARED out the door—leaving it propped open, perhaps to keep an eye on her—Layla rolled out the ball of dough into a perfect circle the same thickness as Justin's sample. He gave the dough a critical once-over when he came back in carrying a tartlet pan, and apparently unable to find fault, demonstrated how he wanted the crust trimmed, and then placed into the pan and crimped for baking.

"Got it?" he asked seriously.

It's not rocket science.

"Got it," she said evenly, sending him a quick, cool glance before turning her attention back to the dough.

"I need fifty. How long will it take you?"

"An hour?" She hoped. That seemed reasonable. About a minute per roll-out.

"Great. We'll bake sixteen at a time. Eight tartlet pans on one of these aluminum sheets." There were two aluminum sheets.

Layla nodded, and then he went back into the kitchen without another word. If she leaned slightly to her left, though, she could see him through the open door, working at one of the counters, pouring cartons of berries into a stainless-steel bowl. He looked so stern, totally closed off. Unlike the laughing guy she'd known for most of her life.

He reminded her of herself.

She shook off the thought and unbuckled her oversize watch.

Okay. One hour. She set the watch on

the counter where she could keep an eye on the time, and started rolling.

Layla was born to follow a production schedule. She finished five minutes early, with a feeling of deep satisfaction, then started to tidy up.

Justin had come into the pastry room periodically to take the large trays to the oven. And didn't say a word.

Preoccupied or pissed off?

Once the tartlet shells were baked and filled, he went back to work frosting the cake, and Layla had nothing to do.

"What's next?"

Justin glanced up at her with a slight frown. "Nothing. I work alone when I frost, and we don't have another function until later this week." He spoke in a distant, professional tone that made her want to take the bottom edge of his white stocking cap and tug it down over his eyes.

He was becoming her. She was becoming him.

And maybe he suddenly had the same realization, because he straightened up and set his spatula on the edge of the frosting bowl.

"Was today everything you hoped it would be?"

"And more," Layla answered easily. "I enjoyed it."

"Rolling dough." He didn't sound convinced.

She folded her arms over her chest and nodded. He mirrored her movement and was about to speak when they heard the office door open and close. Eden called Justin's name.

"Yeah?" he called back.

She appeared in the doorway of the pastry room a second later, a stricken expression on her face. Justin instantly pushed away from the counter he'd been leaning against, and crossed over to her. "What?"

"I need you to take Reggie's place at the function this afternoon." She made a distracted gesture at the cake. "You can do that, right? That can wait?"

"Uh, yeah. Sure."

Layla didn't know what was happening,

but it was obviously some kind of a family emergency. Eden was wide-eyed and pale.

"No. Um. It's…" She looked back at her brother. "Reggie started bleeding. Tom took her to the hospital."

"Oh, shit." Justin pulled his cap off, wadding it in one hand.

"It may not be *too* early for the baby, if they can't stop it. She's almost seven months. They…uh…Tom…didn't know." She swallowed. "I'm sorry I'm babbling." She met Layla's eyes and swallowed again. "Reggie lost a baby before this one."

"I'm so sorry," Layla said automatically. And there she stood, odd man out. With no idea what to do.

"I can be ready in ten," Justin said, moving past her toward the door.

"The coolers are all packed. The van is ready to go. I was just waiting for Reggie." Eden followed him from the room. "Tom will text with updates."

"Are you sure I can't help?" Layla asked as Justin strode through the kitchen toward the lockers near the rear entrance.

Eden turned to her, unshed tears sparkling in her eyes. "Honestly, we're good to go once Justin gets changed." She pressed her lips together. "Sorry to involve you in family drama."

"I only wish I could do something."

"With Reggie out, I'll have to hire a full-time temp, but…" She gulped and then pressed her fingertips beneath her eyes. "If you want to come back tomorrow, if Justin wasn't a total butt today, then do."

"Thanks," Layla said, watching as Justin shrugged out of his shirt and slipped into a chef's jacket. She felt ashamed that, despite the circumstances, she couldn't help noticing he was all muscle. She quickly pushed the thought away and looked back at Eden. "I'll do whatever I can to help." Layla smiled slightly, reassuringly. "I'm very, very good at following directions."

CHAPTER ELEVEN

JUSTIN AND EDEN SLOGGED through the longest, tensest late-afternoon luncheon he'd ever in his life attended. The event progressed smoothly—no minor emergencies, missing supplies, dropped trays, unexpected guests. Only two caterers, smiling frozen smiles, moving like automatons and waiting for a text message from their brother-in-law.

By the time the last guest had left and the cleanup began, Justin was ready to explode. And then the message came.

All's well. Bed rest until end of pregnancy.

Justin felt his chest tighten as a couple big tears rolled down Eden's cheeks. She wiped them away with the back of her hand.

"I'm so glad," she murmured as she gathered a tray of glasses, giving Justin the distinct feeling that if she talked louder, she'd choke up.

He felt the same.

THE VAN WAS ONCE AGAIN parked behind Tremont Catering and was almost entirely unloaded when Reggie's husband, Tom, walked into the kitchen carrying his daughter, Rosemary. Text messages had been flying between Eden and Tom, and Justin had finally been able to relax, but he hadn't expected to see Tom.

"I went to get Rosemary from the sitter's," Tom explained before either of them could ask why he was there. He rubbed his free hand over his dark hair, which was practically standing on end. "Reggie will want to see her when she wakes up." He cradled the child against him as he spoke, his hand coming to rest protectively over the little girl's head. "I saw the lights on in the kitchen and thought I'd stop and get Reggie's laptop." He attempted a smile. "Something to distract her."

Eden reached out to stroke Rosemary's back. "Can we do anything?"

"Just keep my wife out of the kitchen and I think it's going to be all right. She needs to carry the baby for at least another four weeks, although eight would be optimal, and the doctor said with bed rest, it shouldn't be a problem."

"Good to hear," Eden said. "Tell her I'm hiring a temp and that Layla worked out great. She'll come back whenever we need her."

Justin nodded. Resigned himself to working with Layla, and wished he could do something, say something that didn't sound like a platitude. Tom was not a sentimental man, and it was rugged seeing him so obviously torn up.

"This *will* be our last baby." Tom shifted Rosemary so that her head rested more comfortably on his shoulder. She slipped her thumb into her mouth, her eyes drooping as she tried to smile at her uncle Justin, who felt as if his guts were turning inside out. "I couldn't handle losing another," Tom said. "Not at this stage." He cleared his throat. "Not at any stage."

"Two kids are plenty," Eden said. "And this will turn out fine."

Her words sounded totally natural and helpful.

"One good thing," Tom said, his voice still strained.

"What's that?" Justin asked.

"The little guy shifted enough that they could finally get a glimpse at his private parts during the ultrasound. It's a boy."

JUSTIN GOT HOME at the unheard of hour of eight o'clock, although it felt much later. As soon as he arrived he kicked back and blindly pointed his face at a televised game, sans beer.

After an hour of that and another text from Tom, telling them that Reggie had woken up and was feeling much better, Justin went to bed, only to find that without being utterly exhausted, he was unable to sleep.

Tom and Reggie had lost one baby and had just survived a close call on a second.

Justin had let his kid go without a second thought and could still recall the exquisite relief he'd felt when Rachel had decided to put the child up for adoption. His life could get back to normal…except he'd only thought it had.

As an eighteen-year-old, he'd had no clue that later in life he might mourn the loss of a kid he'd never had the chance to know.

You didn't have a choice.

He could have worn a condom.

Amazing how one careless moment could so utterly change a life. Or lives. His. Rachel's. Her parents'. His child's.

It had changed the adoptive parents' lives, too. The only good that had come out of the situation—if they were worthy. That doubt lingered. What if they weren't good people? Wanting a child didn't make a person a responsible parent.

Was his son happy?

Was his son even still alive?

Finally, when he heard his neighbor

who worked night shift come up the stairs, Justin got up, turned on his computer and typed "birth father support" into a search engine. To his surprise, several sites popped up.

He wasn't alone.

He clicked the link to one of them and was taken to a page filled with letters from birth fathers describing their experiences. He'd meant to read only a couple, but an hour later he was still at it. Some of them described unexpected reunions and open adoptions. Some had discovered their children had been abused, which sent another burning arrow of guilt through Justin. Others had found out their children were blissfully happy.

Most of the guys were like him. Men— boys, really—who had been too young to make a decent decision, or without resources to pursue custody of their child. Some had felt loss and pain from the day they'd signed the papers. Some had felt nothing but relief, like him, only to find later, perhaps after the birth of a subsequent child, or in Justin's case a niece, that perspective shifted and it was impossible to forget they had another child out in the world somewhere.

Some guys accepted that adoption was necessary, and others were bitter. Adoption had been Justin's only avenue, because Rachel's parents wouldn't have it any other way and his own father wouldn't stand up for him. Not that it would have mattered. Justin hadn't had the skills to raise a baby.

He had a child no one knew about. Not even Reggie or Eden, who would have blamed themselves for leaving him alone while they both went off to school within a year of one another. Neither of his sisters had wanted to leave him, but technically, their father still lived with them when he wasn't trucking, and hell, sometimes he even came home. Justin had sworn on his life that he would stay out of trouble. No parties. No drinking. Nothing.

And he'd kept his word. His only slipup was with Rachel, the rich girl looking for an opportunity to break free from her controlling parents. He'd had a house and little to no supervision. He and Rachel could spend their stolen time together any way they wanted. And they had wanted to spend it like any other normal redblooded teens.

That all ended when Rachel told him she was pregnant and she was giving up the baby for adoption. The decision had already been made—by her parents. Justin agreed with the decision. In fact, he'd welcomed it with such relief that it made him feel even more guilty.

Rachel had been whisked away to another city to live with a relative, because despite more relaxed social attitudes, her parents could not embrace the idea of their very perfect daughter becoming an unwed mother. So she became a secret unwed mother. And then she probably went off to the Ivy League education her parents had planned for her. Justin hadn't heard from her since. He'd done the occasional internet search, but she must have married, because none of the Rachel Kellys— and there were hundreds—were the right one.

Now he wondered if she felt the same guilt he did. Did she wonder what their child looked like? She had to.

Unlike many of the birth fathers posting in the community threads, he hadn't seen the baby. Hadn't held it or said goodbye. He didn't know, after reading the posts, if that was good or bad. But he did realize that he'd buried his feelings for way too long.

The popular consensus seemed to be that the guys walked off whistling, and the girls were left to deal with matters. He'd done exactly that.

And now he'd give almost anything to undo it…or at the very least, know that his son was all right.

Then maybe, even though he didn't deserve it, he could get peace of mind.

LAYLA ARRIVED AT THE KITCHEN early Thursday morning after phoning Eden to make certain she was needed. Justin's sister assured her they could use an extra pair of hands in addition to the temp who was scheduled to start the next day.

Justin pulled in right after Layla parked, still driving his small Honda, which made her wonder how badly his other car had been damaged in the accident. She should have asked yesterday, but the mood was not conducive to personal questions.

"Hey," she said, keeping it casual.

"Hey back," he said, in a tone that indicated he wasn't interested in conversation. He started toward the entrance to the kitchen without another word.

"Justin?" He'd taken only a couple steps when she spoke, and she easily caught up with him. "Yesterday, after—" she made a circular gesture with her hand, trying to come up with a euphemism for you-shut-me-down "—our discussion, I stayed in the kitchen as a bit of payback, I guess."

He didn't say anything.

"That's not how it is today. I'm just here to help if you need it. As a friend of the family."

"I—we—appreciate that," he said, even though he didn't appear overjoyed. He started across the small parking lot again and she fell into step beside him.

"Although I do wonder why you think I'm incapable of having fun," she couldn't help but mutter.

"I didn't say you were incapable of fun."

"That was the first time I'd ever propositioned anyone," she added. Saying it out loud took some of the sting of rejection away. Made the elephant in the room somehow smaller.

"You did a fine job," Justin said as they reached the door. "I'm simply not in a good place right now."

Why is that, Justin?

Here she'd found a guy who truly turned her on, more so than Robert or any of her boyfriends before him, a guy who'd been around for almost her entire life, and he didn't want to start something.

And for once her shaky self-confidence in personal relationships wasn't shouting, *It's because you're not good enough!* She was. Justin wouldn't have kissed her the way he had—several times—if she wasn't. He'd kissed her because she turned him on—then had planted his heels firmly in the ground and refused to move forward to the next logical step.

He was driving her crazy.

Again.

JUSTIN AND EDEN HAD a quick meeting as soon as he and Layla walked into the kitchen, in which it was decided that Layla would help Eden and Justin would finish his cake. Tomorrow they had a temp starting, coming in for six hours a day, so Eden could concentrate on the office matters associated with the business. There was a debate as to who would deal with prospective clients and meetings, and finally Eden agreed she would be better at that, given the flux in Justin's schedule.

"I called the hotel," he said. "Told them I couldn't come in this week."

"And the temp can give us more hours next week." Eden pushed her hair back as she looked up at her brother. "Will this affect your budget?"

He shook his head. "I'll deal with it." Then, with a quick, unreadable glance in

Layla's direction, he went to his pastry room and shut the door. A few seconds later music came on. Metal from the nineties.

"One of *those* days," Eden said when she headed for the walk-in cooler. She returned a few minutes later with a pan of vegetables. "When he plays that kind of music, he's having a rough one."

Layla was familiar with the feeling, but Justin had always seemed such a cocky, happy-go-lucky guy that until recently she'd never thought of him as having anything but good days. And if he had bad days, she assumed they'd roll off him. So what was all this?

"I hate that music," Eden said. "But we will persevere as we prep. I want you to peel the carrots and onions, then dice them into quarter-inch cubes."

"Sure." The carrots were already washed, so Layla started peeling. Eden began working on celery. Layla had no idea what they were making, didn't really care. She only wanted to help.

"This thing with Reggie and the baby is

rough on Justin," Eden said as she sliced the length of the celery stalks with quick, practiced movements. "He's always been the protector for our family and this is something he can't do anything about. It eats at him."

"I'd never thought of Justin as a protector."

"Oh, yeah. After the old man starting traveling again, he took over the patriarch role in the family."

Layla had always admired the way the Tremont kids had taken care of each other, but she'd assumed that Justin, as the youngest, had been the protected, not the protector. Still, she could see that tendency in him. In fact, it was exactly what he was doing with her—protecting her from his inability to engage in a long-term commitment. As if she needed protection.

"How did Justin end up in the cooking field?" Layla asked. Something she'd vaguely wondered about. "He was such a skating fanatic when he was a kid."

"Once again we can thank our father. We took turns cooking at home while he was gone. Dad made sure we had a decent food budget and we enjoyed experimenting with food." Eden smiled. "Unsupervised experimentation. Justin always liked baking. I think he got a lot of women, using the bread- and pie-making gimmick." Eden sent Layla a knowing look. "Women are suckers for guys who can make a pie, it seems."

Layla gave a soft snort. Yes, she could see where that might work. Especially coming from a guy who looked more at home in a skate park than in a kitchen. The element of surprise.

"Then he got a job helping with a catering firm right after high school, because he happened to be good with the public and made a decent piecrust."

"He got a job because of piecrust?"

"Never underestimate the value of a good crust," Eden said, focused on the garlic. "Anyone can follow a recipe, but there's a knack to having the crusts come out light and flaky every single time. Justin has it."

"Trust me, after yesterday, I'll never look at piecrust the same."

"Reggie and I went to culinary school on loans and grants while Justin was in high school, then he followed us two years later and we started our business."

"And the rest is history."

"So what happened with you two?" Eden asked point-blank.

"I..." Layla cut her a sidelong glance.

"Tactless, I know." Eden started peeling a large head of garlic. "But I had hoped he might find something with you that he hasn't found anywhere else."

Uh... "We didn't even get close to that point," Layla said.

"Well." Eden smashed a garlic clove with the side of her knife. "I figured, given your background, you could skip a few steps."

"Like sharing life stories?"

Eden shrugged. "For one."

She did feel as if they'd skipped some critical steps—the entire middle ones. They'd gone from a fun and promising beginning straight to "it's over."

"I'm sorry," Eden said abruptly, setting her knife down. "None of my business, and Justin would fillet me if he knew I was talking about him, but...this protective thing goes two ways. Actually, three. I guess when you grow up watching out for each other, it's a damned hard habit to break."

WHEN JUSTIN EMERGED from the pastry room to make a phone call around ten o'clock, Layla and Eden were working side by side, prepping vegetables and talking. They glanced up at the same time and both looked first guilty and then coolly indifferent. Oh, yeah. If Guns n' Roses hadn't been so loud, his ears would have been ringing for a different reason.

He ignored them, went back into his lair after the call and once again closed the door. He stayed there until after two, and when he came out again, Layla was gone.

Good. He had a question for his sister, who was pouring batter into mini-quiche pans.

"Were you talking about me with Layla?"

"Maybe." Eden finished one pan and moved on to the next.

"I don't want to seem like a jerk," he said mildly, "but back off." Eden flashed him a startled look as his tone went deadly. "I'm serious. Layla isn't someone I want to play around with."

And why is that? The question was clearly written on his sister's face.

"I don't want to hurt her," he said, saving Eden the trouble of asking.

"How on earth do you know that you'll hurt her?"

"Maybe that was egotistical," he conceded, "but I—"

Eden set down the batter bowl. "Don't do serious. I'm aware. I've watched the pattern develop. Why don't you do serious?"

Justin took a breath, wishing now that he hadn't opened this can of worms. He searched for some easy answer, which didn't appear out of the blue as he'd hoped, and then Eden asked, "Is it because of Dad? Our bizarre childhood? Abandonment issues? What?"

Why couldn't people just understand this one simple fact about him?

"It's me, Eden. Just plain me. No fancy explanations. I like to be single. I only like to let a relationship go so far. I don't want to be responsible for anyone's happiness."

Because I'll surely screw up.

She didn't believe him. He could see it in her face.

Nothing he could do about that.

CHAPTER TWELVE

JUSTIN MADE HIS FIRST post to the birth fathers' group that night. Two simple sentences. How can I find out if my kid's all right? It was a closed adoption. It was a huge move on his part and he couldn't say why, after all these years, he'd finally made it. Maybe the gnawing anxiety had worn him down.

When he pushed Send, his throat went dry. His first actual move to discover something, anything, about his son. Part of him said it was wrong. His son was now someone else's child. Prospective parents were well screened; many waited for years and spent thousands of dollars to get a child. His kid was fine.

Another part of him wanted proof.

A few responses trickled in as the evening passed. Do you have a name? In what state was the adoption made? Have you signed up with an adoption reunion registry?

What he discovered was that without a name and without a state, a search was practically impossible. He had to at least find out where the adoption had occurred. He didn't even know that. All he knew was that Rachel had gone back east.

He'd have to try and contact her parents, find out if they'd mellowed over the years. Not much chance of that. The Kellys had been quite the pair of arrogant social climbers, but he had to try.

They no longer lived in Reno, but he found them in Sausalito, and managed to get an email address of the company Mr. Kelly owned. Justin stopped there. For now. It was going to take some thought to word this message the right way, and even then he knew the chances of getting a response, much less cooperation, were slim.

He finally went to bed—and slept—with no idea if he was going to follow through with any kind of a search, or whether he would continue in birth father limbo.

LAYLA WAS GETTING TIRED of irony smacking her in the face. She'd lived so many long, irony-free years. What was the deal now?

Here she was, attracted to the one guy she'd wanted nothing to do with for over a decade, and he wanted nothing to do with her. Then she'd won an educational merit award—the second in two years—only a matter of weeks after being fired from her teaching job. And now, in a final blow, after pouring two nights into formatting, so that she could put her lesson plans up for sale on The Lesson Store, an online teacher site, she'd received an official, certified letter. Had made a special trip to the post office to get it.

Her heartbeat had gone double time when she saw the name of a law firm as the return address. Skinner, McCullen and Arthur. The lawyers Manzanita Prep used. She knew, because they solicited business once a year at a staff meeting.

If you ever find yourself in a situation where you need legal advice...

Not that teachers were offered a special rate or anything. Layla had often wondered if Manzanita Prep got a cut rate for allowing them to solicit the staff.

With shaking fingers, she tore the envelope open, telling herself this was nothing. Just a formality involved with her nonrenewal/firing/whatever. Nothing to do with breaking and entering. A police officer would be involved if that were the case.

People walked past her on their way out of the post office, and Layla suddenly realized she was standing in the path of a cranky-looking businesswoman, and stepped aside.

Dear heavens…she was being sued for the return of intellectual property to Manzanita Prep. The letter almost slid from her fingers.

Things like this didn't happen to people like her.

Her heart kept beating, somehow, and she read the letter again.

Sued. Or rather, given an ultimatum. Return the lessons or prepare to defend herself.

Layla swallowed drily, then carefully folded the letter and placed it back into what was left of the envelope. Sued. Wonderful. Just wonderful.

Irony at its finest.

REGGIE WAS ON THE MEND. She was allowed to go home from the hospital with the understanding that she was to stay off her feet until the baby was born. Justin had rarely seen his sister off her feet for two hours, much less two months. But Tom was the guy to keep her there.

He spent most of his waking hours at his restaurant, aptly named Rosemary, but had hired a manager that he thought he could trust. Tom was a hands-on kind of guy, and this two months was going to be as difficult for him as it was for Reggie. But he was gladly making the sacrifice. For his wife. And his unborn child.

Layla came in late that day. She'd been there like clockwork at 7:00 a.m. for the past three days, and as promised, she was there to work. Mainly with Eden or the new temp, Charlene, but his sister had client meetings that day, so Justin was holding down the fort and Layla was helping him. Charlene was up to her elbows in manicotti and ravioli prep, and he had a small anniversary cake due the next day and also had to make tiramisu.

"Sorry about this," Layla said as she put her purse into a locker at the back of the kitchen then.

"Are you okay?" he asked automatically, seeing as soon as she turned toward him that she was pale-looking, stressed. The same way she'd looked during finals week every year they'd been in school together.

"Fine," she said in a brittle voice, forcing a smile that did not do her beautiful lips justice. "Just overslept, which I never like to do."

Justin continued to study her for a moment with a slight frown. Something was definitely off. He waited a couple seconds, hoping she'd blurt out whatever the problem was. But she didn't, and he wondered why he wanted to get involved.

He didn't. Of course not. But she was helping them out for very minimal pay—in fact, she'd suggested that she work for free, but neither he nor Eden was having any of that nonsense.

"Where's Eden?" she said, looking around. Charlene, whom she'd worked with yesterday, was rolling out pasta on the other side of the kitchen and the office light was off.

"Client meetings."

"Reggie's all right, then?"

"It's looking good. Every day she lasts is one more day that little Tyler gets to develop."

Layla smiled then, transforming her face from taut and drawn to gorgeous. When had she become so damned beautiful? "They named him?"

"They succumbed," Justin said seriously. Layla's smile lingered for a few more seconds, then slipped away, as if she was recalling something unpleasant.

Which bugged him.

None of his business.

JUSTIN KEPT SHOOTING looks at her. Why? Layla knew she was doing everything right, because she was taking extra care to remain focused. He didn't need to keep checking on her. But he was.

Right now she didn't want to think about Justin—she wanted to obsess over the letter in her purse.

What on earth was her next step?

Why couldn't one of her brothers have become a lawyer? How much of her educational nest egg would she have to spend to defend herself? What if she couldn't afford to go to school?

And how would she ever find a job in education, the only field she was trained for, when she'd been both fired and sued?

Her stomach was in such a tight knot she didn't know if she'd be able to eat. Ever.

"What's wrong?"

Layla jumped at Justin's sudden question, which came from a lot closer than she'd expected. Somehow he was right in front of her, when moments ago he'd been over by his mixer, which was still running. That explained why she hadn't heard him move.

"Nothing." She shook her head to emphasize the point, but wasn't so stupid as to try to smile.

"Right." He reached out to take the spatula she'd been using to scrape batter out of a bowl for cupcakes, which was now dripping onto her shoe. Their eyes met just as Charlene poked her head into the room.

"Hey," she said cheerfully. "I'm done with Eden's prep list. You got anything else?"

"Maybe you could take over here for Layla," Justin said, his eyes fixed on Layla's face.

"I'll finish," Layla said, reaching to take the spatula from him.

He handed it to the temp. "No. Charlene will finish." He smiled at the woman.

"We just need to get these cupcakes in the oven. Layla and I have to—"

With a muttered curse, a word she rarely used, Layla stalked past him, taking her apron off as she went.

This was her last day. She'd come to work at Tremont as a lark, to see if she could gain some kind of insight into her relationship with Justin. And she'd gained instant insight that first day, when he'd explained his position to her. After that, she'd stayed only to help the family she'd grown up with.

They didn't need her now, and she needed to get away from Justin because it was too damned hard being so close to him.

"Layla!"

"Back off," she said without turning around. She dropped her apron on the nearest workstation.

He caught her arm and stopped her. "What in the hell is going on?"

"I'm here helping, but you aren't my boss, Justin. You are not going to call meetings with me or anything like that."

She shook his hand off, opened her locker, grabbed her purse and slammed the door shut again. A few seconds later, she stalked out of the kitchen into the bright light of an early April day. Justin did not follow, and she was so damned glad.

As soon as she got home, she settled at the computer and continued researching intellectual property and copyright. The overall consensus was that she could well be screwed. And if she didn't win the suit, she'd have to pay court costs. Plus she had to pay a lawyer.

She picked up the letter. She had thirty days to answer. Thirty days to either give back the property or have action brought against her.

Would the school honestly go through with it?

Probably.

JUSTIN HAD EVERY INTENTION of driving straight home, but he was worried about Layla, and that concern sent him to the other side of town. He parked in front of

her house, thinking that it looked friend-
lier than it had the first time he'd been
there, steering Layla up the slushy sidewalk.

She opened the door before he got to
the porch, her expression telling him he'd
better stop moving now.

"Why are you here?" she asked coldly
from her superior height.

"Surely you can figure that one out," he
said, lifting his chin so he could meet her
eyes. "Something was bothering you—
to the point that you stormed out of the
kitchen without your sweater." He held it
up for her to see.

Layla rolled her eyes. "That's your sister's sweater."

Justin took a long look at the pale pink
garment. "It is?"

"Yeah. It is." She folded her arms over
her chest.

The hand with the sweater dropped to
his side and Justin went with the facts instead of a ploy. "I wanted to see you, so
I didn't really care whose sweater it was,

but I did think it was yours. I thought I saw you wearing one like this."

"Mine is darker."

"Right." He glanced down briefly, then back up at her. "I've been a jerk. I'm sorry and I'm worried about you." Then he shifted his weight. Apologizing had never come easy for him, but he'd done it and he meant it. Now all he wanted was for her to tell him what the problem was, because it was driving him crazy.

LAYLA DEBATED for all of two seconds, then said, "I'm being sued."

The words just came blurting out. Not because she wanted a shoulder to cry on or anything, but because it seemed counterproductive to alienate one of the few people who might actually understand what was going on—the guy who'd been involved in taking the materials from the school in the first place.

"Sued?"

"Manzanita Prep wants the lesson plans back. They're calling them intellectual property."

"I thought they were yours. That you created them."

"They *are* mine," Layla said adamantly. "But I have to prove I made them on my own time, and that's going to cost money I could use for grad school."

"What are you going to do?"

"I don't know." She wrapped her arms tightly around her stomach and refused to meet his eyes. "It's killing me. I have this problem with authority. I kowtow too much."

"I know," he said softly.

"Authority is safe," she said, still not looking at him, although she heard the creak of him mounting the first step. "I can tell myself that logically I'm in the right, but Justin...people like me aren't supposed to get sued."

"What do you mean, people like you?" he asked, the next two steps creaking under his weight. He stopped on the last one so their heads were level, and when she turned, she could look into his remarkable green eyes.

"People who follow rules. Bend over

backward to follow rules. Follow rules even when they're stupid and counterproductive."

"You do that?" he asked in mock surprise.

She smiled. "Not anymore." Their eyes held, and then she leaned forward so that their foreheads touched.

But she didn't kiss him. Because she knew from past experience exactly what would happen—he would kiss her back and then retreat, for her own blinking protection—and it frustrated the hell out of her.

"I can't figure out my relationship with you," he muttered, clasping his hands at the back of her neck, their foreheads still touching.

Her eyebrows went up. "I think you were pretty damned clear about it a couple days ago."

"No. I was clear about my limitations."

"Why do you have those limitations?" she asked. He leaned away, his hands still on her neck, but his expression had become unreadable, and she could feel the distance building between them. "Do you ever think you can move past them?" she asked in a low voice.

She read the answer in his face before he said it. She stepped back and his hands dropped away.

"We have a history, Justin. You can trust me."

"I know." His mouth tightened briefly and then he leaned forward and kissed her lightly on the lips. She closed her eyes, resisting the urge to kiss him back.

JUSTIN WALKED BACK to his car, heard Layla's front door click shut behind him, and realized that he hated the sound. Hated doors and walls between them. Eden had been right about skipping steps because they knew each other well. But she'd been wrong about them knowing everything, and it was killing him.

The unfortunate truth was that he was falling for Layla. Or had fallen for her somewhere along the line—probably before the awful date at Nia's. Maybe even back in high school, when he'd quit picking on her.

The frightening part was that he suspected, with her, he'd already edged past the bolting point of previous relationships without even realizing it. Somehow the feelings had sneaked up on him and they hadn't even had sex.

Which meant he'd been ignoring the warning signs, for some unfathomable reason, and letting himself slide into something that could well spell devastation in the future.

It wasn't that Justin was afraid to be happy...hell, who was he trying to kid? He *was* afraid to be happy, because the happier people made you, the more it hurt to lose them.

It had hurt to lose his mom. Then his dad. It'd hurt to lose Rachel. And the baby...that was complicated.

The bottom line was that he was flat-out done with loss.

THIS IS CRAZY, Layla thought as she paced through her house. *Let it go.* Justin had made his decision. He wanted to go through life alone.

He says that, and then he kisses you.

She couldn't let it go. She had a stake in this, too, whether he wanted to accept that or not.

What would she have done three months ago? What would old Layla have done?

Maintained distance, because she rarely took risks in personal relationships. Everything was plotted, planned, thought out. Very little left to chance… And then her boyfriend had taken up with her coworker.

So much for old Layla.

New Layla had taken a few chances— and had been knocked backward every time one of them involved Justin. But she was still whole. Still breathing and ready to fight another day.

Therein was a lesson.

She needed to find out the truth, because then she'd know where she stood. Her only concern, after nights of research into the matter, was what if she asked the question and he refused to answer?

Then they truly had no chance at all to explore what she intuitively knew they could have between them, and she would be forced to accept that.

CHAPTER THIRTEEN

JUSTIN WASN'T ENTIRELY surprised to hear the knock on his door that evening. There was no logical reason to expect Layla to show up after he'd brought her the wrong sweater; he simply knew it had to be her.

He opened the door to find her standing there, her dark hair pulled into the ponytail she wore at the kitchen, her features set.

He silently stepped back to allow her to come in, feeling a deep sense of premonition. The bad kind.

"Want to sit down?"

She shook her head. "No. I just have one question for you, and I'm asking it only because I think you need some moral support. You don't have to answer, because, frankly, I have no right to ask."

His stomach instantly knotted. "Go ahead."

It took her a few seconds before she said quietly, "This is so personal, but…" She closed her eyes briefly. "I want to know if you and Rachel might have dealt with something that's affecting your life now."

The bottom dropped out of his world. Just like that.

He swallowed. Or tried to. "Why…?"

Layla's expression was pained, as if it hurt her to ask. "You dated Rachel," she said quietly. "Something about her upset you. She disappeared from high school her senior year, when she was probably in the running to be valedictorian. You've been a wreck about Reggie's baby scare."

"Quite the detective, aren't you?" Every defense he owned had just snapped into place. "And I really don't want to talk about this, Layla."

She swallowed. "The only reason I ask is because you won't let yourself get attached to anyone. Ever."

"Been talking to my sister?" Of course she had. They talked all day long as they worked. "Maybe I just prefer being single."

"I never asked you not to be single. But after we discovered that we, well, hit it off, you backed away from me as if I were on fire."

He didn't know what to say, so he settled for nothing. Talk about being broadsided.

"It's a classic sign of repressed grief," she said. "Not getting attached."

His gaze shot up to hers. "You don't have that psychology degree yet."

Her chin rose in that classic Layla I-know-what-I'm-talking-about expression. "No. But I can read online articles written by those who do have the degree."

"So what's the cure, Dr. Taylor? If Rachel and I did have…what did you call it? Something to deal with?"

She didn't speak immediately, and when she did, her voice was gentle. "Learning to grieve properly."

"Grieve, you say?" What did she know about grieving about something like this? Something secret and unacknowledged.

"My. So easy. And I've been making it so difficult all these years."

She stared at him, unimpressed by his sarcasm, but recognizing a confession when she heard one. He looked away.

"I didn't say it was easy," she finally said.

"Probably because you have no idea what it's like to give up a kid and then spend the rest of your life regretting it. Wondering where he is. *If* he is." He rubbed a hand over the tense muscles on the back of his neck, then dropped it again.

"You have a child."

He didn't dare look at her. "Maybe. I don't even know if my son is alive or dead." He cleared his throat, hoping to keep his voice from getting husky.

"It was a closed adoption?"

"Didn't have a hell of a lot of choice. I asked my old man for help and he told me I'd made my bed and had to lie in it. Famous words from a guy who made his bed, made three kids, then refused to take care of them. I guess he thought I could just write it off, like he did."

Layla took a step forward, but must have read something in Justin's face because she stopped and planted herself there, a few feet away from where he stood.

"And you know what? I did write it off. I was relieved when Rachel chose adoption."

"You were eighteen."

"I… All I can tell you is that I abandoned my child. I hate not knowing anything about him. I think about him all the time."

"You're sure it's a him?"

"It's the only thing I do know. Rachel told me that much when she had the ultrasound. It was a closed adoption. We don't know anything else, won't be able to find out anything until he's eighteen and might try to contact us. Or I might try to find him." No, he'd definitely try to find him. "But what do you say then?" he asked. "How do you explain giving someone up?"

"That you were young and scared?"

"What if he has shitty parents? A rotten life? Think 'young and scared' is going to cut it?"

"What if he's had a great life?"

"That's all I can hope for. But not knowing sucks. Hard."

Layla pushed her hands into her pockets. "Are you in contact with Rachel?"

"Haven't heard from her since she left Reno." He dropped his head for a moment. "I've tried to find her. Through schools and online searches. Nothing."

Layla nodded, and he was thankful she didn't say anything. Didn't flip a few platitudes about it being for the best or anything like that.

"Are you ever going to be able to stop beating yourself up over this?"

"Why would I want to?" he asked coldly.

"Because ruining your life doesn't help anyone else."

Okay. Maybe he'd been wrong about the platitudes.

"Thanks, Layla. I'll keep that in mind."

"Yes," she said with a note of challenge. "You do that."

He looked up, ready to tell her that she couldn't possibly understand, but something in her expression stopped him. Pain. She was hurting for him. Shit.

"My sisters don't know. I just couldn't come up with a way to tell them back then, and after the baby was born, given away, well, it was even harder. So...I didn't. And I would appreciate it if you wouldn't, either."

"I won't tell," Layla said simply. She started toward the door, pausing before she opened it. "But if you ever need to talk..."

Justin tried to look appreciative—his logical brain knew what she was offering. But the raw, scarred emotional side wasn't sharing with anyone. "I hope you understand if I don't take you up on your offer."

"I didn't expect you to," she said candidly. "Because I think you want to keep punishing yourself. But you don't have to be alone in this if you choose not to be."

"No," he said, "I will be alone in this."

"Because it's easier than taking a risk?"

"How in the hell am I supposed to answer that?"

"There is no answer, Justin. Just a seemingly impossible situation." Then she opened the door and walked out onto the landing without another word. He watched her disappear down the stairs, chin up, back stiff. Then he closed the door and went back to the sofa.

FOR THE FIRST TIME in months Justin turned down a cake order, and for the first time ever, it was not because he was overbooked. He turned it down because he was having one hell of a time focusing— on anything.

His secret was not secret.

Layla knew. And because of that he felt…ashamed. As if he should have done more, although he wasn't certain just what he could have done.

But he could do something now. Maybe if he had some answers, he'd feel better.

Whole again. Or as whole as he could hope for.

He had to do something. Whatever he chose to do couldn't be any worse than what he'd done up to now.

Could he tell his sisters?

He didn't know. He'd broken trust by not confiding in them, and now... First he'd see if he could get some answers about the child's well-being, and take it from there.

He'd discovered from posts on the birth father site that he could send a letter to the adoptive family through the agency that had handled the adoption. They could either respond or not. The ball would be entirely in their court until his kid reached eighteen, but Justin had a deep need to send that letter. Explain to his son why he'd done what he'd done.

But he couldn't do that until he found the agency, and the only people who knew the name of it were Rachel and her parents.

Of the two, Rachel was probably his best bet, but no amount of internet searching using her maiden name had turned her up.

Justin paced through his condo, kicked a magazine out of his path, then bent to pick it up and slap it on the coffee table.

Private detective.

Police detective. His brother-in-law was a police detective.

Justin stopped pacing, scrubbing a hand over the back of his neck as he considered. Nick would never need to know why. But if he blabbed to Eden, then she'd probably think along the same lines as Layla.

Couldn't risk it. Right now it seemed as if everyone was looking into his soul, prodding at his secrets. He opened his laptop and punched "adoptive detective" into a search engine. A few seconds later he had a list. He settled on the sofa and started visiting websites with the heavy feeling that he should have done this long, long ago.

LESS THAN A WEEK. Five days. That was how long it'd taken the detective to nail down Rachel's location in Virginia. She'd

married young, attended college for two
years and then dropped out. So much for
her parents' Ivy League dreams. Her husband was a lawyer and apparently brought
in enough for the family to live comfortably.

Justin had an address and a phone
number.

He did not have the name of the adoption agency, which was what his first objective had been. He'd go with the number.

His hands literally shook as he punched
it into the phone. A girl answered and
Justin asked to speak to Rachel.

"May I say who's calling?"

"Uh, yes. Tell her it's Justin."

He'd thought about not identifying himself, trying to trick her into picking up the
call, but he was going to be transparent
about this entire matter. Aboveboard. All
he wanted was the name of the agency so
that he could send a letter. After that he'd
be out of Rachel's life forever.

His heart was pounding as he waited,
wondering if she might just sever the
phone connection, as she'd severed all

other connections. When she answered, her voice was tremulous.

"Justin?"

"Yeah, Rachel. Justin." He felt like saying something trite, such as "long time," but this was too serious. He needed a name.

"How...how did you find me?" she whispered, even though he'd heard her ask the girl to let her have some privacy while she spoke to her "old friend."

"That's not important. I'm not going to bother you. I just want the name of the adoption agency." He cleared his throat. "I want to send a letter to the family. That's all."

There was a choking sound on the other end of the phone, something like a low, keening sob.

"Don't," she said.

"Why? The family doesn't have to respond."

"He thinks Kyle is his father."

What the... "Who is Kyle?"

"My husband."

"Your..." The truth slammed into Justin

so hard he almost dropped the phone. "You…he…" He shook his head, trying to rattle some sense into it. "There was no adoption?"

"I broke off ties with my parents before he was born. They made me choose."

"Then why didn't you tell me?" He would have been there for her. He would have welcomed the chance to be part of his child's birth. Life.

"I'd met Kyle. We decided to raise the baby together."

Justin realized that tears were streaming down his face, running into the corner of his mouth, the taste salty, yet bitter.

"All this time…" He choked out the words.

"Don't ruin this, Justin." Her voice was suddenly calm. Almost harsh.

"What's his name?"

"Justin, please."

"What's. His. Name?"

"I know I handled this badly, but I couldn't let him go. Not after I felt him move. Please, Justin. Please."

"Rachel!"

"Brent. Brenton Kyle." The last word was barely audible.

His son had her husband's name. Cool. Very cool.

Justin blinked against the dampness in his eyes, then clapped a hand over them, wishing he could crawl into the darkness himself.

"He's a happy kid, Justin. Really happy and normal and good at school. Don't ruin this for him. Please, please, please don't screw up his life."

Justin opened his mouth to speak, found no words.

For a long moment neither of them spoke. Then Rachel said softly, "I have done the very, very best I could to give him a great life. Kyle adores him. Brent has two little sisters. Don't destroy our family, Justin."

"Wouldn't dream of it," he finally said.

"Promise me."

"You lied to me and now you want a promise from me?"

"Yes." The word came so softly he barely heard it, but he could hear her swallowing back sobs again. "For him. Do it for him."

"I want pictures."

"Wh-what?"

"Pictures!"

"All right. Give me your address and I'll send some, but you can't contact us again, okay?"

She sounded so damned desperate that Justin almost felt sorry for her. He gave her his email address, then said, "If I find out he is anything but a normal happy kid—"

"I cut ties with my parents to make him a normal happy kid. I sacrificed, too."

"Mo-om." The voice came from the background. A little girl's. Not his son's.

"Justin?"

"I won't screw up your family." He grated out the words.

"I…I am so grateful. You don't know how grateful. I…"

"I get it. Grateful. Goodbye, Rachel. Hug the kid for me."

Then he punched the off button.

CHAPTER FOURTEEN

ONE THING ABOUT a pending lawsuit—it tended to take your mind off other matters. For a few minutes, anyway.

Truthfully, Layla could not stop thinking about Justin, couldn't get his expression of shock and raw pain out of her brain.

She kept trying to tell herself that he would come around. That given time, he'd allow himself to accept help, take emotional risks. But ten years had passed and he'd chosen not to—hadn't even told his sisters about the pregnancy. He'd been building this wall around himself brick by brick.

Maybe that was exactly how she needed to take it down.

One brick followed by another.

But still she didn't act. The old Layla

was taking over, guiding the new. First you put a plan into place. Then you analyze your data. Then you act.

Right now she was analyzing.

There was a time for jumping in and a time for caution.

And there was also a burning need to set things right, but how long was she willing to beat on a brick wall? If Justin had always had a thing for her, as Sam said, then he had every reason to take her up on her offer to be there for him. But he hadn't.

Because he couldn't let himself do that. He couldn't let himself be happy. He faked happy better than anyone she knew, but inwardly, he was anything but. She wanted to see Justin. Shake him. Make him face his grief and deal with it.

All impossible, according to what she'd read.

She needed to forget taking down brick walls, and work on closure. Letting Justin go.

Even if she suspected that she loved him.

She was on her way to her appointment

at the lawyer's office when her phone rang. Her pulse skipped as she recognized the number. Tremont Catering.

"Have you heard from Justin?" Eden asked within seconds of saying hello.

"No," Layla said, stunned at the question. "Not since…" She'd confronted him. "I don't know…Friday night, I think."

"Okay. It's just that he said he was going away for the weekend and that he wanted to take a few days off this week, too. I thought that you two…well, never mind."

That they were off together.

Well, they weren't.

"Did he say where he was going?" Layla asked.

"Since he took all his camping gear out of my garage, I assumed he was going to the cabin. He's been really quiet lately, and sometimes he heads up there when the pressure finally gets to him."

"I didn't know you guys had a cabin."

"We don't. His friend Donovan does. Very rustic. No electricity. No phone. Justin loves it and he's probably there."

"Shorthanded in the kitchen?"

"No. It honestly is a slow week. He couldn't have picked a better time to take a break."

"Sorry I can't be more help."

"I'm sure he'll surface soon. Thanks, Layla."

"No problem." She hesitated one second, then before Eden ended the call, said, "Just one question, if you don't mind telling me…where is the cabin?"

HE WASN'T READY to go back to town. Three days of solitude and most of two bottles of booze had done nothing for him, but he couldn't handle being around people right now. Acting normal, or rather trying to act normal. His sisters knew him too well not to see through his front, and he'd lie to them. Again.

He walked to the edge of the porch, with its view of the postage stamp–size lake, one of many smaller glacial lakes around the larger Lake Tahoe. The cabin was old, had never been wired for electricity or indoor plumbing. Rustic to the max, it was exactly what Justin needed at that moment. Something rough and mean.

The sun sank behind the trees, casting a shadow over the porch, bringing an instant chill. He turned and went inside. It would soon be dark in the cabin, and he debated about whether to light the lanterns or sit and sip whiskey in the dark.

Whiskey had not been his friend the past few days. Apparently the pain was too damned deep to be affected by the booze.

But he took comfort in the fact that even though he'd been lied to, cheated in the worst possible way, he now knew about his son. Not whether he looked like Justin or acted like him, but that he was alive. And apparently happy. Rachel had sounded like a mother tiger protecting her young when she'd spoken to him.

But could Justin trust her? The woman who'd lied to him from day one?

His gut told him that, as much as he hated her right now, yeah, she'd been telling the truth. His brain told him to hire another P.I. to make certain of it.

Once the sun went down, the cabin grew

dark. Perfectly suited to his thoughts, but he lit the lantern anyway and then sat staring out the black windows, then started when lights suddenly cut across the twilight sky.

Headlights?

Donovan was supposed to be in Texas until next weekend, so the vehicle had to belong to someone who'd taken a wrong turn. Justin went out onto the porch, the boards squeaking under his feet. He abruptly stopped when he recognized the car.

Layla walked toward him through the twilight. And something kept him from opening his mouth, telling her to get back down the mountain. That his problems were not her problems.

She didn't speak, either. She mounted the steps, came to stand in front of him, her mouth pressed firmly shut. He could just make out her features in the dim light, but couldn't read her expression. Slowly, she extended her hand, gripping his tightly.

He wanted to ask her why the hell she

was there. Why she was disturbing his solitude, ruining his self-imposed exile. He said
nothing. She led him into the cabin, stopping for a moment to take in the small, one-
room interior. The kerosene lantern burning
on the table cast a golden light over the
cooking area, where he'd set out his camping dishes, stored his coolers of food.

Along the opposite wall was the old
army cot he used as a bed, proudly pur-
chased from the army surplus store when
he was twelve, barely wide enough for one.
His sleeping bag was in exactly the same
crunched up shape he'd left it in when he'd
crawled out with a hangover that morning.

He halfway expected her to say something along the lines of "nice place."

But still…nothing. The kerosene gave
off a faintly oily scent as the burner hissed
away, loud in the utter quiet that lay between them. Then she moved, let go of his
hand and leaned into him, wrapping her
arms around him and holding him until
his arms closed around her. Held her close.

She knew—and apparently she could
accept him, secret and all.

He drew in a ragged breath and then shut his eyes, resting his head against the top of hers.

LAYLA WONDERED if Justin could feel how hard her heart was pounding. She leaned back and slid her hands up under his shirt. His ab muscles contracted as the cool air hit them. For a chef, he was in amazing shape. Probably because he never slowed down. And now she knew why.

His hands closed over hers, stopping her from lifting his shirt farther. That was when she met his eyes, ready to argue if she had to, but she could see he wouldn't. His expression was so heartbreakingly grim, as if he was about to make a life-changing decision.

She wasn't asking for a decision. She was asking for a moment out of time. A connection. Healing and closure for her. But she didn't have to argue, after all, because instead of talking, Justin started unbuttoning her blouse, working one-handed, releasing each plain white button on her plain white oxford blouse with a simple twist of his fingers. She'd debated about borrowing more seduction wear from Sam, but decided against it. This wasn't about seduction. This was about healing. An act of love with no strings attached, no commitment required.

She needed to give to Justin without asking for anything back.

He lifted her hand and undid the cuffs, first one and then the other. The shirt slipped off her shoulders and dropped to the rough plank floor, followed a few seconds later by the beige cotton bra that had offended Sam so deeply. This time Layla shuddered from the cool air. Justin pulled his T-shirt over his head and for one brief moment they stood toe to toe, bare to the waist. His eyes were on her breasts as he brought his hands up to caress them, weigh them in his palms, his thumbs moving over her peaked nipples. She shuddered. A very good shudder that started somewhere very deep inside her.

That was when Justin finally spoke. "Cold?" he asked softly.

Layla simply nodded.

He took her hand, led her to the narrow cot. Let go of her to unzip the sleeping bag, folding it open. By the time he was done, Layla had kicked off her shoes, slipped out of her jeans, removed everything except her panties. When he turned back to her, he stood for a moment, hovering on the brink. She could see he was starting to rethink things, but she wouldn't allow that. Not now.

Not when she needed him as much as she sensed he needed her.

When he opened his mouth, she touched it gently with her fingertips and shook her head. Justin took the hint and started to unbutton his Levi's. When he pushed them down over his hips, his erection sprang free, quelling any doubts she had about mutual need. She stepped out of her panties and eased into the sleeping bag, arranging herself on her side so there was room for him, too. He went to his wallet, which was lying on an overturned wooden box, and pulled out a condom before he climbed in beside her, and then they were flesh to flesh. The de-

licious sensation of being close to Justin's
hard body triggered a rush of heat.

He shut his eyes as he pulled her even
closer, his hands smoothing her back
down to the curve of her hips, then up
to her breasts. She returned the favor,
loving the feel of his hard flesh under
her palms, reveling in his sharp intake of
breath when she circled his erection with
her fingers and stroked to the tip. Once,
then twice.

He reached down to stop her, then tore
open the condom with his teeth. Layla
took it from him and slowly unrolled it
over his erection.

His mouth found hers as he moved her
underneath him, nudged her thighs apart.
She wanted to tell him to take his time,
understanding intuitively that this might
be the only chance she got to make love
to him. Who knew if he could ever break
free of his self-imposed burden of guilt
and punishment?

He supported himself on his elbows,
and Layla sensed that he needed to be
inside her. Now. He needed the release,

and she'd give it to him. And as he pushed in, slowly, maddeningly slowly, she gasped against his shoulder.

She was making love to Justin, former scourge of her life, and she did not want it to end anytime soon.

Justin obliged. He moved in her so very slowly, pulling out, then easing back in, pushing himself to the hilt, hitting all the spots Layla needed hit, bringing her so close to the edge that she started to clench her hands. And then pulling back, taking away the pressure, only to start the slow build again.

He stroked her hair as he moved, kissed her deeply, and then seemed to disappear into himself as his movements came faster. Layla didn't care. She was there to give, to make love to him, and then she, too, got caught up in the sensations of her own body, moving with Justin, meeting his thrusts with her own until a cry caught in her throat and she pressed her open mouth against his shoulder just as she felt him shudder, empty himself.

Layla still had nothing to say. This was enough. Just being. Here. With Justin.

LAYLA FELL ASLEEP not long after they made love, nestled half on top of him, since that was the only way they could both fit under the sleeping bag. Justin stroked the flat of his hand idly over the smooth skin of her back and arm, occasionally letting his palm slide down to the curve of her ass, then back up again, feeling his body start to respond.

She was so beautiful.

And he was so damned messed up.

He hadn't intended to fall asleep, but woke up when Layla tried to ease over him. He caught her by the waist and held her there. Her startled expression shifted as he began to grow hard again. Maybe they'd talk. In a while. Right now he just wanted to lose himself once again.

LAYLA GOT OUT OF BED and started collecting her clothes, shivering in the chill air as Justin worked to rekindle the fire in the barrel stove, which had gone out while they slept.

"Why are you dressing?" he asked.

"I'm leaving," she said.

"No. It's too late."

She smiled tolerantly. "I'll text when I get back."

He rose to his feet and crossed over to her. "So this was a hit-and-run?"

She gave him a long, steady look and continued to button her shirt. "I have to go."

"Why?"

"Because I told myself I would do this only once. If I stay, I'll do it again."

"Would that be so bad?" he asked quietly.

Layla forced herself to concentrate on the last of the buttons. "No. But it isn't going to fix anything, either. Unless you want to fix things." She looked up. "I love you as you are. I've done my very best to just prove that to you. You don't love yourself and that's going to stand in our way."

He opened his mouth to argue, then

closed it again, perhaps because there wasn't an argument he could make. She'd spoken the simple truth.

"I was up-front about that."

"Yes, you were. And I'm also being up-front." She went to him and put a hand on his chest, felt his heart beating against her palm and wished things could be different.

"I'm sorry this happened to you, Justin. I'm sorry you had no support system when you needed it." She let her hand drop before she lost her willpower, and went to pick up her jacket off the wooden chair.

I'm sorry you won't accept help now.

"If I could offer you more, I would," he said as she slipped into the jacket and lifted her hair over the collar.

"Good to know." She felt the distance between them, distance she'd put there. Maybe she was selfish for wanting to sleep with him once before walking, but she didn't regret it. "I have to go."

She lost the fight with herself and crossed the room to where he stood, stone still, and pressed a kiss to the side of his face. "I wish things could be different," she said in a low voice. "But they aren't."

And showed no sign of changing in the future.

"I hired a guy to find Rachel." He blurted the words just after her lips touched his face. She practically froze in the act of kissing him.

"Have you found her?"

Justin's expression became hard. "I found out that Rachel kept our son."

For a moment Layla couldn't speak. Couldn't find her voice. "She kept him?"

"My son thinks her husband is his biological dad."

"Are you going to do something about it?" Layla demanded.

"No." Justin took a few steps closer to her, and she could now see the battling emotions in his eyes. Pain, frustration. Sadness. "Rachel broke off with her parents, probably because she met the guy she was going to marry, and he helped her. They had the baby and raised it as their own."

"She kept him and never told you?" Layla felt a groundswell of fury. "You've been going through hell and she's been giving birthday parties and experiencing milestones." Layla found herself blinking back tears. Tears of anger, tears of empathy.

Justin reached down and took her hands, which she hadn't even realized were balled into fists. The hell that woman had put him through!

"She was trying to protect him. Give him a father."

"He had a father," Layla said.

"I meant one in the same family." Justin looked down at her. "I keep asking myself what I might have done had positions been reversed. If I'd had the kid in my hands, had a chance to raise him with someone I loved, what decision would I have made?"

Probably one that wouldn't have destroyed anyone's life.

"I've never held a kid of my own," Justin said, "but I've seen Reggie and Tom with theirs, and I don't know that I could have given him up if I had."

"But surely you would have told the other parent."

"Not if I'd wanted that child to believe he was being raised by his two biological parents."

"Are you going to be able to forgive her?" Layla finally asked.

"I don't know." He rubbed a hand over his forehead. "It's not feeling too good right now, and that worries me."

"Why?" she asked softly.

"I have feelings for you, Layla, but I've been messed up for a while. A long while. I want to come to you whole." His mouth worked for a moment before he said, "I'm not there yet."

She tilted her chin up. "It doesn't matter."

"Why?" he asked.

"You're whole enough for me. The rest we can work on together."

"But don't you see, Layla? I'm not whole enough for me."

CHAPTER FIFTEEN

JUSTIN SHUT UP the cabin shortly after Layla drove away, hurt and frustrated because he wouldn't, or couldn't, let her help him. That seemed to be her perpetual state around him. It killed him to keep doing that to her, but regardless of what she said, he wanted to come to her a whole man. Not some shell of a guy with deep problems. Not a bitter man, angry at what he couldn't fix. So angry at Rachel that he couldn't allow himself to think about what she'd done.

Why would Layla want to hook up with a guy like that? A guy who, as she said, had nothing to give back. No sane person would do it.

He'd just pulled into his driveway when his phone rang in his pocket. He hoped it was Layla, but it wasn't a number Justin recognized, nor was the voice. Masculine with a note of stress in it.

"Justin Tremont?"

"That's me," Justin answered in a flat, don't-try-to-sell-me-anything voice. He stared out his windshield at the bushes in front of his parking spot.

"I'm Kyle Linnengar. Rachel Kelly's husband."

Justin had the oddest sensation of his face going numb as the blood drained out of it. "Yes?"

"I'm calling because…" The guy's voice trailed off, the emotion in it clear, even though he was trying to hide it. Put on a brave front. "My wife is not doing well since you called."

"I haven't been doing well for the past ten years."

There was a brief silence before Kyle said, "I can fully understand that, being a father."

Justin closed his eyes. Okay. Acknowledgment. Kyle had unwittingly played the proper card. When he didn't answer, Kyle continued.

"I...I need to know what your intentions are in the future, so I can prepare my son."

"I don't know," Justin said honestly. "He apparently thinks you're his dad."

"I *am* his dad," Kyle said in an adamant voice. "But so are you." He spoke as if he needed to placate Justin, so as not to rile him into action.

"And like Rachel, you're asking me to disappear?"

"For Brent's sake, I am."

"I already told Rachel I wouldn't destroy your family."

"It *would* do some serious damage to our family if you came into Brent's life, but I understand why you would feel the need to do that."

"Damage your family?"

"See Brent. Only...I'm asking you not to."

"He's a pretty happy kid?"

"Totally happy. He's a kid kid, if you know what I mean. The kind that skateboards off the roof."

Damn. Was skating off the roof a genetic tendency? "Has he done that?"

"I caught him in the planning stages." Justin once again felt moisture welling in his eyes. "I know how hard this has to be. It's hard for us, too, not knowing what you're going to do. Living with this shadow over us. I don't think Rachel has slept through the night since you called. My daughters keep asking her what's wrong. But I know that's not your concern. We made the decision to do this."

"I don't get why she didn't tell me."

"She wasn't in a good place. Her parents insisted on the adoption. We met when she was six months pregnant. I worked at the clinic part-time as an office aid during my first year of college, and we started talking while she was waiting for an appointment. We kind of fell in love and…well, imagine two eighteen-year-olds in a forbidden love situation. We married. Kept the baby. And, crazy as it is, it worked out."

Up until now.

"I want a picture of him."

"I, uh…"

"You can email it to me. Just…a picture. I need to see him."

"I can do that," Kyle said. "And then what?"

"And then," Justin said, his throat closing, "I think that's it. You'll raise your son."

Kyle cleared his throat. "If you give me the address, I'll see what I can find to send."

"Thank you," Justin said. "And tell Rachel…look, I'm not going to lie. I'm mad as hell, but I won't hurt the boy. Hurt your family."

"All right."

"One more thing."

"Yeah?"

Justin cleared his throat. "If he happens to come up with any ideas regarding bikes and ramps over fences, make him wear a helmet."

"Will do."

After giving Kyle his email address, Justin paced through the house, fighting the urge to start beating his fists on the wall. There wasn't a lot he could change here. Fair? No. Reality? Yes.

And he recalled Layla's words about not taking away from anyone, but not giving, either. He wasn't giving anything back. Nothing permanent, anyway.

He was just existing. Feeding his grief, refusing to give anything more than he absolutely had to. True, he wasn't taking more than he was offering…unless he counted Layla. He'd taken something from her. Freely offered, but if she hadn't cared deeply for him, hadn't been hurting because of him, then she wouldn't have lit into him as she had.

Wouldn't have understood him the way she did.

An hour later he checked his email, and sure enough, there it was, waiting for him. An email from the Linnengar family with an attachment.

His hands actually shook as he opened the messageless email and clicked on the attachment. The photo loaded slowly, starting at the top of a blond head and moving down over blue eyes, Justin's eyes, to a freckled nose—Rachel's—to a gap-toothed grin. Definitely some mischief there, and a kind of sweetness he hadn't expected. Brenton Kyle Linnengar smiled out at the world with a happy, trusting expression.

It appeared that his son was doing just fine without him.

LAYLA TRIED ON the green dress she'd worn on her less than stellar date with Justin, and slipped a short cream-and-black Chanel-style jacket over it. Three weeks had passed since she'd left him at the cabin, and no contact. It appeared their moment together was over. It'd sure be nice if she could shove him out of her head. But that was the way Justin had always been— there when she didn't want him to be.

"Not bad," Sam said, leaning back on Layla's bed. "Maybe a couple gold chains and you're good to go. Although I can't believe you really are going."

"I've won an award. I'm going." Not looking forward to it… No, she was in one way. She was looking forward to doing what no one thought she would do—accept her award. How could she not?

"Would you like some company at this event?" Sam asked as she got off the bed and started digging through Layla's meager jewelry cabinet. She pulled out the one and only gold chain, held it up, then shook her head.

"Are you volunteering to go to a boring awards ceremony?"

"No. I'm volunteering Willie again." Sam put the gold chain back and came out with a heavier silver one. "He won't sing. He promised me."

"Maybe you could go?"

"Sorry. I have a lingerie party booked tomorrow night." The parties were Sam's latest endeavor, and had taken off like a rocket, or perhaps a Rocket Launcher—still her top-selling item.

"Kind of short notice for him, since the ceremony is tomorrow," Layla said.

"He'll be free," Sam said with certainty.

Layla let out a sigh. "I would love to

have Willie escort me. Perhaps you could ask him to pick me up at six?"

Sam smiled. "I already have."

LAYLA WAS NOT AT HER HOUSE. Justin walked back to his car, wondering if she was at the library or a class or something. He'd tried to call first, but her phone was off. That was when he'd decided to do what she'd done to him over and over during the past several weeks, and simply show up at her door.

She definitely had more success doing that than he did.

Maybe Sam's shop. If she wasn't there, he'd call again.

The door was locked, but he could see Sam's red head bent over as she counted out her cash drawer. He knocked on the glass and her head snapped up. She frowned, then crossed to the door.

"Well," she said simply.

"Yeah. Uh, I was trying to find Layla."

"Call her."

"I think her phone is off."

Sam rubbed her head with the hand

holding the money. "Probably is." She shrugged. "Guess you'll have to wait until tomorrow to do whatever it is you're planning to do."

"I wasn't going to do anything but talk." And talk. "Why tomorrow?"

"She has that educational awards thing tonight at the convention center and won't be home."

"Shit. The Merit Awards." He frowned. "Convention center?"

"She has a date," Sam said sternly.

Great. He forced a smile. "Thanks."

WILLIE ARRIVED AT LAYLA'S house five minutes early. He'd cropped his beard and wore a suit jacket over a dark glen plaid shirt. Since he was six foot four inches tall and solid muscle, he looked a bit like a CEO lumberjack. Layla smiled at him.

"Thanks for doing this, Willie."

He cleared his throat. "I don't mind. I owed Sam."

Layla slipped into her coat and grabbed her purse. She'd known Willie for almost five years. He and Sam had once been lovers, but now they were more like best buddies.

"I hope it was for something big," Layla said with feeling. "Or else she's going to owe you."

"Is this thing going to be boring?" Willie guessed.

"So boring that you'll want to be shot and put out of your misery. But the food is pretty good." Or it had been the time she'd won the award for her Civil War class.

"I brought my phone. I can play games under the tablecloth."

"Would you do me a favor?" Layla asked. The idea had come to her that morning. Tonight was going to be the perfect meshing of her old and new selves. The plan had been made, but it would take chutzpah to carry it out. Both old and new had a job to do.

"Sure," Willie said. "Name it."

"I need you to move some stuff for me."

JUSTIN ARRIVED at the convention center wearing his best catering suit, after deciding the catering tux would be too highbrow for this affair. He'd been mis-taken—there was everything from tuxes to corduroy blazers—but his suit fit nicely into the range of fashions worn by the short line of people about to give their tickets at the door.

Tickets.

That could be a problem—or it would have been if he hadn't worked this facility so many times. Justin did an about-turn and headed for the kitchen. He walked in as if he knew what he was doing—which he did. He was crashing a teacher party by looking like a caterer.

No one questioned him as he headed out the service door and then stepped aside to stand next to a set of curtains. Every table was full and it took him a while to find Layla in the darkened room, wearing the same green dress she'd worn the one time they'd gone out. She was sitting next to a giant.

A few weeks ago Justin would have said he was not a jealous man, but he knew now that was not true. He was jealous. And he wanted that big guy gone.

ONCE THE DESSERT DISHES had been removed and the opening remarks began, Layla had the uncomfortable feeling she was about to hyperventilate. The opening remarks lasted about twenty minutes too long, as they always did at educational functions, but it gave her time to finally spot Ella across the room, sitting with Dillon and his wife, Dora James from the math department, Tom Galliano from social sciences and his wife, and Melinda. Representing the English department, no doubt. Sans Robert.

Hmm. Trouble in paradise? Darn.

Layla drew in another deep breath and then jumped when Willie put his big hand over hers. "Relax," he said, in what was probably supposed to be a whisper.

"Trying," she said.

There were only twenty recipients of this award, statewide, and, thanks to low airfares from Las Vegas to Reno, most of the winners were actually present. Plus there were school board members, administrators, legislators and fellow teachers showed up for the meal and to show support. The room was packed.

Once the actual ceremony started, the teachers took the podium, received their award and said a few words. Or, being teachers, a lot of words. Witty, warm and heartfelt words. Her friend Dillon's speech made her tear up as he talked about the excellent students he was privileged to teach.

She probably wouldn't get a chance to teach again after tonight.

When it was her turn, she walked up to the podium, climbed the two steps, took her award, faced the audience. And then she nodded at Willie and the big man got to his feet.

"I want to thank you for this award," she said. "But it's not mine." She pulled in a breath as the audience went silent. "I discovered that the lessons that won me this award are not my property—according to Manzanita Prep, anyway. I am being sued for their return, even though I prepared them on my own time and paid for the materials myself. And it all came out of here." She touched her head.

There was a low muttering in the audience. Ella sat stone still almost directly in front of Layla, staring straight ahead, unaware of Willie coming up behind her, carrying a heavy box. It probably was good that Sam had sent her big friend instead of coming herself.

"But," Layla continued, "I have to prove that, and frankly, I don't have the funds for a legal defense. Therefore—" there was a loud thud as Willie placed the box on the table between Ella and Dillon, then dusted his hands and started back to his seat "—I am returning the lessons to Manzanita Prep, where I hope they get good use, and perhaps someone else can win an award for them. I'd also like to note, for the record, that the materials have been returned by the required date set forth in the legal documents sent to me." She smiled and held up the award. "I'll also see that Manzanita Prep gets this, too, since they've done so much to deserve it."

JUSTIN WAS WAITING on Layla's porch when she got home, accompanied by her giant escort. She stopped dead in the middle of her sidewalk when she saw him, pressing a hand against her chest, and Willie instantly moved around her, lumbering toward him in a menacing fashion.

Justin scrambled to his feet. He hadn't foreseen this and it sounded like the guy was growling.

"Willie, I know him."

The big man stopped and looked over his shoulder. "Yeah, but do you want him here?"

Layla nodded wearily. "Yes. Unfortunately, I do."

Justin adjusted his lapels as Willie turned back toward Layla. Justin might not have been able to take him in a fair fight, but he could have outrun him.

Layla solemnly put a hand on Willie's shoulder. "I now declare you released from whatever hold Sam has over you. Thanks for helping me tonight."

"Cool." Willie clapped Layla on the shoulder in return, then lumbered to his car, humming "Yellow Submarine" under his breath.

And then it was just the two of them. Facing one another over a long length of concrete sidewalk, Layla near the gate, Justin near the porch.

"I told my sisters," he finally said.

"And?"

"It was emotional."

"I can imagine."

She drew in a soft breath, momentarily dropping her gaze. "Or maybe, in all honesty, I can't. But I'm glad you did it." She looked up at him hesitantly. "Do you want to come in?"

"Yes." More than she could say.

Layla gave a slight nod, then turned to silently unlock the door.

"Are you doing okay?" she asked once they were inside. "After…everything?"

"Better than I have been." He reached out to take the coat she slipped off her shoulders, draping it over the back of the basket chair. "I will never be Brent's dad. But I know he's safe and happy with parents who love him. That has to be enough."

"Can you let that be enough?"

Justin nodded. "I'm not saying it will be easy, but…whole or not…I have to form new relationships. Or bolster up the old ones in my life."

"Yeah?" she murmured.

"So anyway, I thought I'd come tell you that."

Her eyes flashed, letting him know that he could breathe. All would be well. "Thanks for the update," she said stiffly.

"And that you were great tonight."

Her mouth fell open. "Great…?" She cocked her head. "You were there?"

"Yep. I guess you might be getting that master's in psychology now?"

"I narrowed my options with that stunt, but you know what? I don't care. I like psychology."

Justin took a few slow steps forward. "And you're pretty damned good at it."

"Really?" she asked softly.

He stopped in front of her and reached out to touch her hair, then trail his fingers down her cheek. Her eyes drifted closed momentarily as she leaned into the caress. "I think you know you are."

"Anything else?" she asked as she put her hand over his.

"Only that I haven't had a real relationship since Rachel. Not one that was headed anywhere." He caught her fingers in his. "I want to try to make a relationship now. If you haven't given up on me."

"Justin..." She shook her head, holding tightly to his hand. "I can't say it hasn't been tempting, but try as I might, I haven't been able to do that."

He kissed her then. Touched her lips slowly, gently—that was the plan, anyway. But the kiss got away from him as heat flared between them. They were both a little breathless when he finally lifted his head.

"It isn't like I didn't try to help."

"You did make a good effort." She leaned back to look up at him. "But it wasn't good enough. Somehow, for some crazy reason, I still love you."

EPILOGUE

BRENT'S TREE WAS almost two feet tall. Justin had planted it as the smallest of saplings, so small that he didn't know if it would make it, but it had weathered the Nevada heat in Reggie's backyard along with the trees she'd planted for each of her two children. Now, midwinter, it was once again a bare little twig, but he could see the neophyte buds already formed, ready to burst forth next spring.

Layla had helped him pick it out—an apple tree—and together they'd prepared the spot, planted the tree.

Justin told her that when they had children, they'd plant another. And another. And another.

She'd laughed and told him not to buy too many trees.

He'd sent Kyle, Brent's father, one last

email, telling him how much it meant to him, knowing his son was happy. Kyle had sent back a brief response, thanking him for the heads-up about the ramp—a message Justin had printed out and tucked into his favorite cookbook.

Rituals seemed to be the key, because now he was coping. And Layla was by his side, coping with him.

They'd made one promise to each other the night he'd come back—issues would be confronted instead of buried—and Layla was now pursuing her psychology degree with a vengeance. Justin never thought he'd spend so much time quizzing someone, but that was how he spent many of his evenings. Either that or with Layla perched on the stool in the catering kitchen, studying while he worked on his cakes, offering the occasional suggestion.

And for the first time in over a decade, Justin felt at peace with himself, at peace with the world.

Funny what love could do to a guy.

* * * * *

LARGER-PRINT BOOKS!
GET 2 FREE LARGER-PRINT NOVELS PLUS
2 FREE GIFTS!

Harlequin

Super Romance

Exciting, emotional, unexpected!

YES! Please send me 2 FREE LARGER-PRINT Harlequin® Superromance® novels and my 2 FREE gifts (gifts are worth about $10). After receiving them, if I don't wish to receive any more books, I can return the shipping statement marked "cancel." If I don't cancel, I will receive 6 brand-new novels every month and be billed just $5.44 per book in the U.S. or $5.99 per book in Canada. That's a saving of at least 16% off the cover price! It's quite a bargain! Shipping and handling is just 50¢ per book in the U.S. or 75¢ per book in Canada.* I understand that accepting the 2 free books and gifts places me under no obligation to buy anything. I can always return a shipment and cancel at any time. Even if I never buy another book, the two free books and gifts are mine to keep forever.

139/339 HDN FEFF

Name	(PLEASE PRINT)

Address		Apt. #

City	State/Prov.	Zip/Postal Code

Signature (if under 18, a parent or guardian must sign)

Mail to the Reader Service:
IN U.S.A.: P.O. Box 1867, Buffalo, NY 14240-1867
IN CANADA: P.O. Box 609, Fort Erie, Ontario L2A 5X3

Not valid for current subscribers to Harlequin Superromance Larger-Print books.

**Are you a current subscriber to Harlequin Superromance books
and want to receive the larger-print edition?
Call 1-800-873-8635 today or visit www.ReaderService.com.**

* Terms and prices subject to change without notice. Prices do not include applicable taxes. Sales tax applicable in N.Y. Canadian residents will be charged applicable taxes. Offer not valid in Quebec. This offer is limited to one order per household. All orders subject to credit approval. Credit or debit balances in a customer's account(s) may be offset by any other outstanding balance owed by or to the customer. Please allow 4 to 6 weeks for delivery. Offer available while quantities last.

Your Privacy—The Reader Service is committed to protecting your privacy. Our Privacy Policy is available online at www.ReaderService.com or upon request from the Reader Service.

We make a portion of our mailing list available to reputable third parties that offer products we believe may interest you. If you prefer that we not exchange your name with third parties, or if you wish to clarify or modify your communication preferences, please visit us at www.ReaderService.com/consumerschoice or write to us at Reader Service Preference Service, P.O. Box 9062, Buffalo, NY 14269. Include your complete name and address.

HSRLP11B

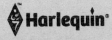